Noelle's Rock 3

By

Theresa Hodge

D0066873

Text **LEOSULLIVAN** to

22828 to join our mailing list!

To submit a manuscript for our review, email

us at submissions@leolsullivan.com

Legal Notes

Thank you God! I've made it to book number 3 in this series. Without you, I couldn't have done it. All thanks to you for the strength and the ability to see my project through.

This is for you daddy…The rock of the Bickerstaff clan. Rip.

To all of my readers, ne
w and old. I want to thank each of you for taking this journey with me. I want to give a special shout out to a wonderful Veteran Author, Miss Francine Craft, for taking the time to encourage me and extend her knowledge. I would also like to thank Captain Roberto Simmons, for sharing his knowledge of law enforcement with me. May God bless each of you with the strength to endure whatever may come. May he bless you to receive all the many blessings, he has in store for each of you. Remember, together we stand…divided we fall. Keep the faith and keep love flowing always…

Yours Truly,

Theresa Hodge

CHAPTER 1

Beau

"Breathe baby, breathe!" I coach Noelle as the doctor orders her not to push just yet. My heart swells as I see my love lying there preparing to bring a beautiful part of herself into the world.

"I want to push now!" Noelle screams as sweat drizzles down to her brow.

I quickly swipe the sweat away with the back of my hand. I kiss her cheek and say, "Sweetheart, you have to wait and do what the doctor tells you to do."

I love Noelle and I know she is in pain, but my world would crush if anything were to happen to her during this delivery. Therefore, even though she is looking at me like she wants to punch me in the face, I have to admonish her to do as the doctor asks.

The delivery room doors swing open and in rushes Shelby like a breath of fresh air. Boy, am I glad to see her. I have someone else who will help me talk some sense into Noelle.

"I'm sorry I'm just getting here, but traffic is murder out there today, and it is moving at a snail's pace," Shelby says as she stops at the hand sanitizer machine by the door and presses the button. She is rubbing her hands together as she approaches Noelle's bed.

"All that matters is that you're here now," Noelle says between pants as she reaches her free hand out towards Shelby.

"How is the little mama doing?" Shelby asks me.

"She's doing great, aren't you sweetheart?" I ask Noelle, giving her a boost of encouraging words, even though she's been acting like she's about to lose it ever since she started having contractions.

"Alright now. Noelle, on the count of three, I want you to push," the doctor advises as the beginnings of another contraction shows up on the monitor.

I bend down and place a kiss on Noelle's sweaty forehead. She looks like an angel lying there with her hair scattered about and the grimace of childbirth on her face. All I want is for our baby to be healthy and for Noelle to be happy.

"One, two, three," the doctor's counting cues me to hold Noelle's leg up as she prepares to push.

It takes thirty minutes of constant stopping and pushing before the most beautiful eight-pound, seven-ounce, twenty-two-inch long, little baby boy enters this world. I am in complete awe as I watch the doctor suction his nose and mouth. When he starts to cry, I smile, while squeezing Noelle's hand. "You did it," I mouth to her.

"Dad, do you want to cut the cord?" the doctor asks, breaking me out of my thoughts. A special moment that I hadn't even dreamed of happening was interrupted by commotion out in the hallway.

"Sir, you can't go in there!" a female nurse yelled.

"What the hell?" I say when the delivery room doors bursts open and I'm staring Noelle's ex, Victor Wallace, in the face.

"Am I too late? Please tell me I made it in time to see my son be born?" Victor bursts in as if he has every right to be here and starts talking about his son. The same son that he broke up with Noelle over and told her that he wanted her to abort.

A nurse rushes in apologizing for Victor gaining access to the delivery room. "Doctor, I am sorry. I tried to detain this man. Do I need to call security?"

The nurse looks at Noelle for an answer to her question. But, if I have anything to do with it, security won't be necessary.

"Get the hell out of here, Wallace. You have no business being here," I said, stepping away from Noelle's bedside and toward Victor.

"I have more business here than you do!" Victor says. He looks over the doctor's shoulders and, in that moment, the baby lets out a squeal.

"Yes, get security," the doctor says to the nurse. "Daddy, are you ready to cut the cord?" the doctor asks, looking in my direction.

"Yes," Victory and I both say, stepping toward the baby.

"I'm the daddy, so it's my duty to cut the cord," Victor says in a demanding voice.

"Victor, stop it!" Noelle says. She sounds flabbergasted at the nerve of Victor showing up suddenly wanting to be the man he should have been in the beginning.

Everyone else in the room, including Shelby, is stunned by Victor showing up. I am furious as I take the scissors from the doctor, turn my back to Victor and cut my baby's umbilical cord.

A nurse takes the baby from the doctor to clean him up. I watch until the baby is securely placed in a small bed on the opposite side of the room. I glance at Noelle who looks as if her heart is heavy. How dare Victor come in here and ruin one of the best days of our lives? I strip off my gloves and throw them aside.

"Beau, No!" Noelle's scream falls on deaf ears as I charge in Victor's direction, ready to rip him a new one. "Wallace, didn't I tell you to stay the fuck away from my wife! How in the hell did you get through security anyway?" I ask him between gritted teeth.

"That's my baby in there and the woman that I love," Victor yells out angrily.

Blood rushes to my head and I begin to lose all reason. He dares to lay claim to my woman and my baby, after throwing them away like yesterday's newspaper. I don't think so.

"Beau!" I can hear Shelby call my name. All I can think about is beating Victor's face to a pulp.

"Stop it! The both of you," the doctor shouts in a loud, demanding tone. "This is neither the time nor the place for this type of behavior."

My back is to the doctor and my anger is too far gone for me to take heed to his reasoning.

"You better listen to him," Victor says with an evil glare in his taunting eyes. "That baby is mine and you have absolutely no business claiming my son. Noelle and I made our baby together and, if I have anything to do with it, we will raise him together."

"You will do nothing of the sort!"

I charge straight towards Victor, like a bull seeing a red flag dangling in front of it. Victor throws up his arms like a defensive lineman blocking a defensive back, but I dip to the side, push Victor's elbow down and away. I grip his head in a headlock. I pay no heed to the excitement and loud voices around us. I roll Victor to the floor, which is no easy feat, since we are both muscular men.

Once full body contact is made, I begin to pound Victor's face with my fist. I take out all of my bitter anger on the man that impregnated my beautiful angel, then threw her away to fend for herself. I beat him for not being the man he should have been for Noelle in the past and I beat him for ruining what should've been the most wonderful moment between husband and wife. He is a fucking asshole for showing up here today and I am going to give him something to remember this moment.

"Stop it, Beau! Noelle needs you," cries Shelby with a teary voice.

"Damn you to hell, Victor."

I ignore Shelby's pleading voice. I now have a death grip around Victor's throat and, if I squeeze just a tad harder, I will surely kill him. Blind rage has taken me to a place that I rarely ever go. I feel no pain, when Victor quick jabs me in my face, trying to deflect my grip from his corded throat. I concentrate solely on inflicting pain on him. My hands are like an iron vise around his neck and I won't be satisfied until Victor expels his last breath. I can hear running feet in the hallway, before I feel a hand at my shirt collar, trying to force Victor and me apart.

"Let him go!" a man's voice orders.

"Let go of me!" I force out between gritted teeth as I struggle to hold on to Victor's neck.

"What the hell is going on here?" A voice booms from behind me. "Get your hands off my son or I swear by God, I will have your job," states my father.

"Oh, my God!" I hear mother's voice cry out. "Beau, stop it, we didn't raise you to behave like this. Noelle needs you to be level headed right now."

"Beau," Noelle's voice is the only voice that penetrates through my mad haze. My hands lose their grip around Victor's neck. I fall back and away from Victor. I breathe in and out heavily, trying to catch my breath. My father reaches out his hand in an offer to help me to my feet. I allow him to assist me, before turning towards Victor.

He is lying on the floor gasping for air. I watch as he tries to get up on his own, but he fails miserably. Two security guards lift him to his feet. He stands there and glares at me with hatred. I glare at him with equal hatred, for there is no love lost between the two of us.

Victor's stance still holds defiance as he struggles to catch his breath. "You will pay for this, Beau Barringer. Mark my words, the day will come that you will regret the day that you put your hands on me. I can promise you that!"

"Get him the fuck out of here!" I order the two security guards.

"Yes sir, Mr. Barringer. Look man, it's Beau Barringer," one of the guards said to his partner.

"Aw man, we didn't realize it was you, Mr. Barringer! We will remove this man, right away," his partner said.

"I don't know how he even made it to this floor. He didn't come pass us on the elevator; I can promise you that," says the first guard, giving me a star struck look as he walked over to Victor. "Sir, we're going to have to ask you to come with us," the guard said to Victor.

"How the hell are you going to automatically take his side?" shouts a disgruntled Victor before he understands that I clearly have the upper hand. "Oh, you are going to pay for this Beau Barringer. I promise you will pay! Everything you think you've stolen from me will one day be mine again. I swear this on my life!" He yells with a crazy look of a lunatic in his eyes as the guards surround him.

"Just get him the hell out of here!" I order. I'm so angry that fury radiates through my voice.

"Like I said Mr. Barringer, I'm really sorry. I'm one of your biggest fans. We will get this dude out of here. Do you want to press charges?"

"Your wife's blood pressure is through the roof! All of you out of here now!" the doctor orders, cutting in through my contemplation of pressing charges against Victor.

"Just get him out of here!" I order once again.

"This is some shit right here," Victor mutters beneath his breath, but I don't have the time or the patience to give him any more of my attention. Noelle is my number one priority. I don't know how I allowed him to get under my skin enough to lose sight of her wellbeing.

"I need Beau," Noelle's weak voice reaches my ears once again.

"Come on son," my father urges me to leave the room and do as the doctor instructs.

"No!" I need to stay with my wife. She needs me. My baby needs me," I say in a desperate attempt to force my way back into the hospital room. Minutes ago, I was begging Noelle to do what the doctor asked and now I am faced with the same dilemma.

"Beau, we have to do what the doctor asks. You don't want to be barred from the hospital, do you?" asks Shelby with tears in her eyes.

"That's right son. Listen to Shelby and the doctor. Once they get Noelle's blood pressure under control, they will allow you back inside."

"Father, she needs me," I say looking over my father's shoulder, at a pale faced Noelle."

My eyes meet hers before the door is firmly shut in our faces. My mother, father and Shelby all stand around wondering if Noelle and our baby are going to be alright. I feel helpless standing on the outside of the delivery room, while my wife may be fighting for her life on the inside.

CHAPTER 2

Victor

After Leaving The Hospital

"Fuck! Fuck! Fuck!" I beat my head against the plastered wall, until I can feel the wetness of blood trickle from my forehead. I pay the copper smell of blood no mind, for my thoughts are on the way I was treated when I went to the hospital to be with Noelle and my baby boy. Beau Barringer made a fool of me once at the Christmas carnival six months ago when he got all up in my face about Noelle. Now he suckers punches me good and got the best of me this second time. I promise you it won't be a third time I fume to myself. Thank goodness I put this plan in motion when I did, because white boy won't know what hit him. That will teach him to mess with me! All these fucking thoughts continue to run through my aching head a mile a minute. All of my hatred for Beau is finally coming to a head.

"Let's see who has the last laugh now rich boy! After all these months of my careful planning and strategizing, I will have what rightfully belongs to me. There is no fucking way that I will allow Beau Barringer to raise my son. I don't give a damn if he is a rock star. That is my son, not his!" I scream aloud in the silence of the apartment that Noelle and I once shared.

I feel nothing but anger and hatred for Beau Barringer. I wish he was dead.

With darkness burning in my soul, my booted feet walk silently but deadly across the carpeted flood. This is the same floor Noelle and I laid upon on a numerous of occasions to make love, whenever we didn't make it to the bedroom.

My beautiful Noelle…

How did I allow her to slip away from my grasp? The err of my ways are beating me as rapidly as my beating heart. I snarl aloud when I think of how Samantha played me. She and her husband now have my son halfway across the world. My hand clenches in frustration at the thought of her and her husband reuniting, after the promises she made of us becoming a family. Instead, she follows her husband to Japan, when he accepted a promotion to head up a new electronic start up company. I hate her and, if she was near, my hands would be wrapped around her fucking throat by now. I can just imagine watching life ebb out of Samantha's body slowly…oh so slowly. She is the reason I lost my beautiful Noelle.

The ringing of my cell phone interrupts my thoughts.

"Speak!" I say into the receiver, not caring who is on the other end of the phone call.

I listen to the caller carefully. I don't want anything to go wrong with the plan I decided to go ahead and set in motion after my fight with Beau Barringer.

"Are you sure you have everything I need?" I ask the caller. I pause and listen, before I speak again. "I will leave the key where you can find it. It will be above my door, taped to the frame. You will have two weeks to finish the job...no more. Leave my key inside, when the job is done." I say and listen to the caller's gravelly voice reply.

"Great!" I can feel elation building on the inside of me like a fever. "I can't have a paper trail that leads back to me," I reveal to the caller.

"I will be sure of it, sir," the caller assures me.

"I want everything tailor made to the diagram I have drawn up," I instruct him. I cease speaking to listen to the caller's reply once again. "Good! Once you finish with the construction; remember, I will need for you to destroy everything that will lead back to me or you. And I need at least three months of supplies. I will email you a list of all of the particulars that I need. Delete the email afterwards...I must stress to you about us not leaving a paper trail," I warn the caller again. "Your money will be at the drop off, where we previously agreed upon. After you receive your money, forget you ever knew me and disappear. As long as everything is done to my specifications everything is good."

I listen to the caller's assurance before I begin speaking again. "I have a lot of work to do but first things first. I need to make sure all of my work is caught up at the office, since I'm going to be away from the office for an extended period of time. I have a room at a hotel until you're finished with my plan. I will be in touch," I add before ending the call and putting the caller to the back of my mind.

I have a lot to do and such a little time. I'm lucky that I'm in a position to work from home. The work that I do in the office can easily be done from home. All of the extra hours, I've been putting in at the office, will finally pay off. I'm due so much paid time off that I am able to cash in enough to get three months of my salary. This amount should be plenty to pull off what I'm planning to do.

I walk over to the mirror and look at the prints from Beau Barringer's hands around my neck.

"Motherfucker, you will pay. I promise on my life that you will regret ever taking Noelle and my baby from me!" I say aloud.

The blood from my forehead his slowly drying. One day soon, I will see Beau Barringer's blood drain from his lifeless body. A bubble of laughter begins to rise in my chest and works its way out of my mouth. I throw back my head and boom out with laughter. My laughter can be heard loud, clear and demented throughout my otherwise quiet apartment. A place that was home to my Noelle and can be again. Even if it has to be over her husband's dead body.

CHAPTER 3

Beau

Six Weeks Later

"No, that's not going to work for me, Dave," I said, shaking my head at Dave's request.

"Beau, your career is at its all-time highest. How is it going to look, for you to back out of all of your commitments now? That's not a professional look, and I haven't gotten you this far by being unprofessional." My music manager, Dave Dillinger, tries to make me feel guilty, so I will come around to his way of thinking.

I take a deep breath an exhale. Dave is telling me the truth. I signed off on this deal long before my whirlwind romance and marriage to Noelle happened. And, any decision I make not only affects Noelle and I, it also affects the livelihood of Dave and my band members. That is what makes this decision so much harder.

"Plus, if you don't do this tour in Europe, it will affect your future bookings and you can and will be sued for millions. Are you ready to take a liability hit such as this, Beau?" Dave questions me with a pleading look in his eyes. "Please don't ruin your career and the members of your band, by thinking with your heart. You have to use your business acumen to stay on top of this game. For Christ sakes Beau, your family owns a multi-million dollar company. You don't need me to tell you how this game is played," Dave continues to nail his point home.

My head wars with my heart. Noelle isn't going to like me being away from her for a whole month. My schedule will be more grueling than it ever has been before and she will unlikely be able to even get in touch with me some days, while I am away.

"Dave, is there a way I can do the tour without Courtney?" I ask the question, even though I already know the answer.

"Beau, you know better than to ask that question. The making of your last album is what has led to this very moment. Man! This tour is going to make history and set your career in stone. You have got to do this. I promise you nothing but gold from here on out. Have I ever led you wrong?"

I have to admit there is truth in Dave's words. He has never led me or my band wrong. He is one of the best managers in the business and I am blessed to have him as part of my management team.

"Okay, Dave, you've convinced me. But please keep the announcement of our upcoming tour out of the media…at least until I talk to Noelle. This decision will get me in the dog house for sure. Especially considering the kiss that happened between Courtney and me the last time we were together."

"Do you need me to talk to Noelle? I really like her and she is truly a sweetheart. I think she has won everyone's heart that is connected with you, in some way or another. I will explain to her the politics of the music industry and selling albums. You have to give the people what they want to stay on top," Dave continues with his extensive knowledge.

"I know what the music industry entails, Dave, so I can explain it to her. But please always know that I'm not going to sell my soul to this music industry. I stepped down from my dad's company and broke his heart to follow my dream. Although we've moved past that now, I can't forget how I disappointed my dad. I'm just glad my little brother Hunter stepped in to pick up the reigns. What I'm basically saying is that I don't have a problem with choosing what is important to me. If I have to choose between my lifelong dream of having a music career or Noelle, I will, without a doubt, choose my wife."

Dave acknowledges the hard, serious look in my eyes. He raises his hand in understanding. "I get what you're saying buddy…I really do. There has got to be some type of medium established to please the wife without ruining your career."

"We will see. Like I said earlier, just give me time to talk to Noelle tonight. I will give you my definite decision on tomorrow. Then and only then, can you release the tour dates and cities to the press."

"I got it man. Whether you believe it or not, I really admire your dedication to Noelle and the baby. You are one good man, Beau Barringer. I'm not only lucky enough to be your manager, but I'm honored to call you a friend, as well," he says patting me on the back. "Now let's get back to the rest of these contracts, shall we."

I hurry through the reading of the contracts, which my personal lawyer has already read over and given me the go ahead to sign, before heading home to Noelle and baby Brandon. But before I head home, I need to meet with my brother, to get some things off my chest.

CHAPTER 4
Beau

"How is everything going brother?" Hunter asks, before sitting down at the bar in an exclusive club in Upper East Manhattan.

"Everything is going well, so far."

"I'm glad you called me to meet up with me. We are long overdue for some brother hang out time. I know you're a married man and all, but we still got to have our guy time," Hunter teases.

"You're right and everything is going well, so far," I reply and signal for the bartender, so Hunter can place his drink order.

I have a serious frown on my face. I'm not my usual relaxed, jovial self and I have a line of shot glasses lined up across the bar in front of me to help cheer me up.

"It looks like more is going on than meets the eye, Beau," Hunter says, gesturing toward the line of shot glasses. "Are you drinking all of those? If so, you're going to be smashed by the time you make it home to Noelle."

"The way my day has gone, I need it," I state, before taking another shot to my lips. I grimace at the burning effect of the alcohol as it slides down my throat. "I'm far from drunk though," I add.

"Has Noelle's ex-boyfriend come around trying to start trouble between you and Noelle again?" asks Hunter, after telling the bartender his preference of drink.

"No, we don't see or hear anything from him. It's almost like he's walked off the face of the earth. Shelby tells me that he's taken an extended leave away from the office."

"Shelby is a regular source of information. How did she come across this bit of information?" asks Hunter.

"She has an acquaintance that works in the same building where Victor is employed. Shelby's acquaintance is friends with his secretary, it seems."

"That's great. Out of sight out of mind, I suppose," Hunter replies in a doubtful tone of voice.

"I hear the doubt in your voice, Hunter. I'm doubtful when it comes to Victor too. This is why I've taken liberties and had some papers drawn up by my lawyer for Victor to sign. My lawyer sent them over by courier. I can't just sit back like Noelle and do nothing," I say.

"What kind of papers?" Hunter asks.

"Paternity papers that ask him to relinquish all of his rights as the father of Brandon, so that I can adopt him as my son."

"And does Noelle know that you have those paternity papers drawn up by your lawyer?"

"No, I didn't mention anything to Noelle about it," I admit with a shrug to my shoulders. "I had paternity papers drawn up, on my own. I have to protect my family at all cost. Besides, I don't want Victor to be a bigger of a problem in our lives, than he already is. I can tell the incident in the hospital still worries Noelle, although she doesn't want to talk about it. Every time I bring up the subject of her ex, she doesn't want to talk about it, not even to her best friend Shelby. It's like she wants to bury her head in the sand and forget it all happened. I even asked her to file a restraining order against him, but she says no. She seems to think a restraining order will just set Victor off and make things worse," I said. "Man, I just don't understand her."

"I think that's a great idea about having the paternity papers drawn up. I also think a restraining order will be a great idea," Hunter agrees. "In all reality, Noelle and the baby is your family now. I can't believe he asked her to have an abortion and then turns around and wants to play the father of the year. Men like him are scum," Hunter adds, before taking a sip from my drink.

I take a look at my little brother who was once a womanizer himself and feel pride swelling up in my chest. Madison must really be doing him some good.

"I can't agree with you more, little bro. Victor needs to sign over his rights over to me and let us get on with our lives. I want to give Brandon the Barringer name. I didn't produce him but he's in here!" I say, placing my hand over my heart. "I want him and my future babies to bare the same name. There won't be any difference between this child and our future children. All will be treated and loved equally."

"Hopefully, he'll be sensible and just sign the papers, bro," Hunter said, after taking a nice swig of his drink.

"I don't want to have to revert back to beating the crap out of him again," I say with venom dripping from my tone. No one moves me to anger quicker than Wallace.

"Wow, I don't know what to tell you, Beau. You are in a precarious situation, when dealing with another man's child. The best you can hope for is for him to sign those papers and get the hell out of your life. If you need me to have a talk with him, I'm more than ready to do so. I don't like seeing my family fucked over for anything," says Hunter.

"If I thought our problems would be solved by you going over there and roughing him up a bit, I would say hell yeah, go for it. But I don't want you involving yourself in my problems. You have your hands full with your new fiancée," I say with a smile.

"You're right, Madison is a hand full, alright." Hunter smiles and the love he has for Madison resonates from deep within. "I'm not trying to change the subject or anything, but how did you keep that fiasco of you fighting with Victor out of the press?" he asks.

"My lawyer and publicist were on it before Victor stepped out of the hospital. The hospital had everyone sign confidentiality clauses or they risked losing their jobs if they say something about the incident. We even had the entire hospital shut down for a short time. Victor wasn't supposed to just be able to walk up into the delivery room in the way he did. Before Noelle was admitted, we had a list set in place of the people to be allowed in, so after a few threats that I would damn sure make good on, the hospital complied with everything we asked," I say and rake my hand through my wavy black hair. I release a frustrated breath and take another gulp of my drink.

"What else is worrying you Beau? I got a feeling there is something more on your mind than just Victor."

"You know me well, don't you?" I ask, looking at my younger brother with a half grin.

"Of course, I do. There isn't anyone, except maybe now Noelle, who knows you better. Now tell me what's bothering you besides that ass wipe Victor Wallace."

"My manager has informed me that it's in my best interest to do the tour in Europe."

"The one you signed on for last year," Hunter asks.

"Yeah, I signed off on it before Noelle entered the picture. This was all set in motion before I knew, Noelle, my beautiful winter angel, existed."

"How much money is on the line and what are the repercussions you will have to deal with, if you don't follow through with the contract?" my brother asks, his ever present business mind is on alert.

"We're talking about losing millions and millions in ticket sales, appearances and endorsements from other businesses," I admit. "That along with lawsuits. There is no legal way around my obligations," I add.

"Noelle will understand. She seems like a reasonable and smart woman. She had to know what she was in for when she married you."

"She is reasonable and smart. I just don't know how reasonable she will be when I tell her that the tour will include me being in close contact with Courtney Nicks. It's the album we did together last year during the holidays that we will be promoting."

"Ahh, now I see your point. You just have to be honest and straightforward with her. Let her know the business end of the outcome, if you don't fulfill your contractual obligations. Noelle wants the best for you. That woman loves you, Beau. I'm sure she will understand and trust your loyalty to her, as well. How long will you be away this time?" Hunter asks.

"I hope you're right about Noelle understanding and trusting me. Because, I will be on a month-long tour."

"A month-long tour with Courtney Nicks?" Hunter looks at me with pity in my eyes.

I can tell from the look in his eyes that he knows Noelle will blow a gasket for sure. It's not that much trusting in the world, for a wife whose husband will be around an ex for that length of time.

"Why are you looking at me like that, Hunter?"

"What way? I'm not looking at you in any kind of way. That's just your imagination," Hunter says quickly.

"Uh-huh, right. You can lie to me with your mouth, but your eyes can't lie. I know what you're thinking. You're thinking that I'm going to be in for some deep shit, when I tell Noelle of my plans."

"Those are your words big brother, not mine," Hunter says. He shakes his head and looks away from me and to the big TV screen hanging on the wall behind the bar.

"You didn't have to say a word," I say. "Your expression says it all."

"Okay! I don't envy your position one bit. Noelle isn't going to like you being around your ex-girlfriend for that long. But if she trusts you like a wife is supposed to do, she will be fine," Hunter says in an encouraging voice.

"Bullshit!" I say.

"Bullshit, is correct. Let me be truthful. There is no way in hell Noelle is going to be happy about this tour, but you have to go and fulfill your obligation. Noelle has the whole Barringer family now. We will keep an eye on her, and Shelby, I'm sure, will too." Hunter sounds assuring, but I still at a loss.

"Damn, I hate to leave Noelle so soon after the baby arrived. Brandon will be another month old before I get to hold him in my arms again. How can I go a whole entire month without sleeping with my wife, kissing her or holding her in my arms? This shit is crazy. I've never felt this way before…" I quit mid thought and my voice trails off as I contemplate about my dilemma.

"I tell you what, let's drink to getting Victor Wallace out of you and Noelle's life sooner rather than later. Let's also drink to the chance that, by some miracle, your wife will take it easy on you and not give you hell." Hunter raises his glass in the air and I raise mine to clink against it.

"I will drink to that. Now, I need to get home to my beautiful wife." I sit my glass on the bar's counter and stand up. I remove a couple large bills from my wallet and lay them on the bar area. "You stay a while and drink up. Drinks are on me, little brother. And also thanks for the pep talk. I really need it."

"Anytime Beau, and thanks, big brother, for the drinks. Give Noelle and Brandon my love."

"Will do," I say, before taking my leave. Noelle and I deserve all of the happiness that life has to offer. I will move heaven and earth for my brother if I can. And I know without a doubt, he will do the same for me.

CHAPTER 5
Noelle

I look down at Brandon as he is sleeping in his baby bed. I can't believe how fast time has flown by. My little baby just went for his six-week checkup exam earlier today. His chubby cheeks look adorable as he sleeps.

"He looks just like you," Beau says as he walks into the nursery to stand behind me. His strong arms encircle my waist. I can smell the scent of alcohol on his breath when he places a soft kiss against my cheek.

"You think so?" I ask with a glint of joy on my face. I look up into my husband's adoring sapphire blue eyes and can't believe he's my husband. I can't believe Beau even surprised me with this mansion in an affluent Upper West Side neighborhood in Manhattan. We are in the midst of twenty other celebrity homes and we live closer to his family now, so that's a plus, especially since Beau is big on family. He even, from time to time, alludes to the fact that he wants to meet my mother and stepfather. He wants me to make peace with my family.

Since marrying Beau, I've fully come to the realization of what kind of family I married into. Even before Beau followed his dream of music, he ran a multimillion dollar family company alongside his father. This way of living will take me a while to get used to…if ever. Beau not only has money from his career, but he also owns a large percentage of stock in his dad's publicly traded company.

"Of course, I think so," he answers softly, his voice pulls me away from my quiet thoughts. Beau uses a soft voice when speaking, so he doesn't wake our sleeping infant. Yeah, I have a sleeping infant. I get excited just thinking about the fact that I'm a mom. "I'm sorry, I didn't make Brandon's six-week appointment with you today. The meeting with my manager held longer than I thought it would," he informs me, with disappointment in his eyes.

"Don't worry about," I say before taking one more look at our baby. I bend to place a soft kiss on his chubby cheek. I double check to make sure the baby monitor is on before turning to take Beau's hand in mine and walk out of the room.

"After leaving the meeting, I decided to meet up with Hunter at the bar. I had a couple of drinks with him before coming home," Beau says.

"How is Hunter, by the way?"

"He's great. He sends his love to you and Brandon."

"That's sweet of him. I really like Hunter…Speaking of your brother, I', having lunch tomorrow with Madison and Shelby."

"That's great baby. I'm glad you have such good friends in those two," he replies.

"So am I, I agree…Are you hungry?" I ask him, since he's just getting in.

"No, we ate at the office. Did everything go well with Brandon's exam? I know you had your six-week exam today too. Is everything okay?" he asks.

A seductive smile spreads across my face. I know Beau really wants to know if it's okay for us to make love. "Everything is perfect," I tell him. "I still have twenty pounds to lose before I'm back to my pre-pregnancy weight," I admit.

"I don't see a problem with the extra weight. In all honesty, you look sexy as hell with the extra weight," Beau replies, with a sexy arch to his brow.

"You just like it because my butt is bigger," I tease him.

"You damn right," he replies and begins pulling me into our bedroom. He closes the door behind us. "You're sure everything is fine with your health?" He questions me again. "You gave me a fright, when your blood pressure was spiked the way it did during your delivery."

"You know the cause of my blood pressure shooting through the roof like it did. I can't wrap my mind around the way Victor acted that day. He was like a different person," I say to Beau.

The look in Victor's eyes disturbs me every time I remember the way he looked at me that day. But I keep this part of my thoughts to myself. I don't want Beau to worry any more than he does already. He hardly wants to let me out of his sight as it is. But a red-flag warning is going off in my head about Victor. I push it into the furthest recess of my mind, when I look into my husband's heated gaze. It has been much too long since we've been together intimately. I miss him and I know undoubtedly he misses me too.

"Baby," Beau drawls out, in a deep husky voice, as he walks up behind me.

"Hmmm," I respond and lean my head to the side as he nuzzles the side of my neck with his heated lips. I can feel the silky hairs of his neatly trimmed moustache and beard caressing my skin.

"You know how much I've missed making love to my wife. I think I've developed a case of everlasting blue balls," he says with a laugh.

I shudder when his tongue licks from the side of my neck to my jawline.

"I've missed tasting all of you," he murmurs against my ear. The hotness of his minty breath brushes against my flushed sensitive skin. "Damn it, I'm like an addict awaiting his next fix."

I can feel Beau's hardness against my ass but I'm nervous since this will be our first time making love since me giving birth. My entire body starts to tremble as he continues to stand behind me. My wild curls have fallen in my face, shielding the blush that has arisen on my cheeks. He turns me in his loose embrace and his mouth doesn't waste any time with capturing my lips beneath his. He slowly drags his lips away from mine and look deep into my eyes, before speaking.

"Baby, I promise to be gentle. I won't hurt you," he tries to put my mind at rest as if he is reading my thoughts. "Do you trust me my love?"

I nod my head yes without opening my mouth to speak. Beau's magmatism is drawing me under his spell. I trust my husband with every fiber of my being. Beau's head dips and I close my eyes readying myself for the feel of his lips against my on once again.

My mouth immediately opens up for him. I'm so ready to receive his hot kisses. I allow him dominate possession and I love it. His hands are like hot irons touching my body and heating it wherever he touches. He touches me gently but his strokes are sure. He knows every curve and dip to my body. He also knows every imperfection but he loves all of me. This I have no doubt of.

"You have on too many clothes," he grunts sexily against my lips.

"You do too." I agree with him.

"We can rectify that together."

He ends the kiss reluctantly by stepping away from me. I instantly miss his lips being against my own. But it's not for long as we divest one another of our clothing with haste.

I stand before him nude. My breasts are heavy and my nipples are hard and throbbing for him. They seem to beg of him to capture them between his kissable lips. His lustful gaze takes in every inch of my body. My eyes, in turn, take in all of him…every delectable inch. His taunt six-pack abs tease and beg me to reach out and touch. His fine, silky hairs on his chest rise as if they are electrically charged.

"Bed. Now!" He growls out in a playful tone of voice.

I walk over to the bed. In truth, I float as if I'm on cloud nine, over to the bed, from Beau's direct order with the biggest smile that a woman can have attached to my face.

"Baby, lie back on the bed," he urges me. "I'm going to make love to my beautiful wife you now. Get ready," he speaks in a low gentle growl.

I climb to the center of the bed and lie flat on my back. My legs lift and I spread them spread far apart. Beau eases a large fluffy pillow under my ass for my comfort. I can feel the moistness from my pussy, already seeping down the side of my thighs. My pussy is calling to him…silently but most surely. His sweet words and his loving actions has me mentally fucked already. My nervousness is slowly disappearing bit by tiny bit. It's silly how I almost feel like a virgin getting ready to make love to my husband for the first time.

My coily curls falls to one side of my shoulder as I watch Beau walk toward me. His nine inch cock with the deep purple veins riddling inside his smooth velvety skin, leads the way towards his destination. He lick his lips and watch me with deep intent, before he climb onto the bed behind me.

Beau lifts my feet and kiss each of my toes before drawing my big toe in his mouth. His eyes never leave my own as he seduces me further under his erotic spell.

"Who loves you sweetheart unlike any other?" He asks me as he slowly kisses his way tenderly up my calf towards my thigh.

"You do," I gasp out in a small voice as he kisses his way slowly toward my moist center.

"That's right, you better know it," He mutters with placing his face directly in front of my fleshy slick heat. "Now it's time for your husband to feast...Feed me, baby."

I moan aloud when he begin to eat me out. My head falls back on the cushiony pillow with a soft thump. My whole entire body becomes weak from the pleasurable sensations running through my core. His tongue pries my slick pussy lips apart to tantalize my clit. "Beau! I've missed this," I whimper.

"You've miss me tasting my delight, huh?" He chuckles sexily against my throbbing mound.

"Yes!" I sob, aloud. Beau's ministrations are bringing tears to my eyes.

My answer seems to give Beau the extra incentive to dine as if he is dining on a five star meal.

It takes everything in me, to hold my position and not squeeze his head in a death grip between my thighs. He lick my clitoral hood in long slow strokes. He slowly suck my now sensitive clit into the warmth of his mouth. I cry out my thankfulness. He lick my labia before darting his stiff tongue into my wet sticky love tunnel as he fucks me as if he is fucking me with his shaft.

"I'm cumming Beau," I wail out in pleasure and coat his tongue with my essence. Beau continues to lap at my heat until he licks up all of my juices. He rises before I can catch my breath and sheaths his hardness slowly into my slick heat.

He slide his hands under my ass and slides me closer to him. I can feel him holding his strength at bay. He keeps his words and make love to me slowly and gently. I fall even more in love with my husband with each pleasurable tender plunge of his hard steel. My ass pushes back at him with each of his forward thrusts. He holds me at the waist to adjust my movements to his tempo. His pulsating cock is causing a pleasurable burn inside of my heated walls.

"I love you, Noelle," Beau grunt out in a thick voice laced with desire.

"I love you too, Beau," I gasp in surrender to his pillage of my body.

Beau's every touch and kiss orchestrates me delightfully under his mastery. I know no other man will have my body or heart like my husband today and always.

"Cum for me Noelle," Beau growl near my ear," before he plunges his tongue into my ear canal.

My pussy throbs and blooms like a rose petal opening up for the sun. I tremble and cum with my husband's iron of steel embedded deeply inside me.

"I'm cumming, sweetheart," Beau's husky voice reaches my ears as he splatters his seed deep within me. I am lucky the doctor has given me a Depo-Provera shot, or Beau will be impregnating me again with the amount of cum that's he's spurting inside of me.

I give feel it starting to drip down the side of my thighs as he is still plunging inside of my soak walls again and again. He gives one last plunge, before he fall back onto the bed and pull me into his strong muscular arms. It's not long before we both are lured into a weakened exhausted lust fill haze onto the soft bedding…drowsy with the effects of our lovemaking.

The baby takes this moment to cry. Beau is instantly alert as he place a soft kiss against my neckline. "I'll go and see about Brandon. When I come back I want you to be ready for round two. I have a lot of making up to do," he says before biting one of my ass cheeks. I am sure by the pressure of his bite, he leaves a mark.

I raise my head drunkenly in time to see Beau don a robe, before opening the bedroom door and walking out of the bedroom. I smile brightly to myself. I am feeling more loved by my husband, day by day. I am one blessed woman, I think to myself, before getting off the bed to walk to the adjoining bathroom to the large glass enclosed shower. I adjust the water to a comfortable temperature before stepping in to await Beau. I am sure the lovemaking will resume shortly, when Beau return. I sigh aloud and basks in the after effects of Beau's loving.

CHAPTER 6
Madison

"Noelle, I want to thank you and Shelby for including me in your luncheon date.

"Girl, don't worry about it. You are very likable with a pleasant personality. It's a pleasure in getting to know you," Shelby says.

"Shelby is right, Madison. It's also great to have someone around that I knew back in Georgia. I don't have too many pleasant memories as you know…Even though we weren't close in school, I always thought you were a nice person," says Noelle, speaking of our past.

Suddenly Noelle gets a frown on her face and looks around the busy restaurant.

"What's wrong?" Shelby and I ask in union, when we see uneasiness appear in Noelle's eyes.

"I don't know," she visibly shudders and rubs her hands up and down her arms as she hugs herself. "It feels as if someone is watching me but I never see anyone," she divulges.

Shelby and I looks around the restaurant as well. But neither of us see's anything out of place.

"Maybe it's your hormones kicking in," suggests Shelby.

"I'm not going through depression or having mood swings Shelby," I sighed. "I've been feeling like someone's watching me ever since my wedding day."

"I know you jest!" Exclaims Shelby. "Why are you just telling me this? Have you talked your concerns over with Beau?" Shelby questions Noelle as if she's the CIA.

"No, to both of your questions."

"And why not?!" Shelby gets loud.

"Because Beau will only worry too much. I don't want him to worry about me," responds Noelle.

"Of course he worries about you, Noelle. He's your husband. I think its sweet how protective he is of you," I chime in.

"Speaking of being protective, how are your grandmother and mother dealing with you being so far away from them?" Noelle asks me.

"Listen to Noelle trying to get all off subject. We are talking about you now," says Shelby. I still want to know why you haven't told Beau, about your concerns. I don't like it one bit!" She exclaims.

I notice Shelby is like one of those little dogs with a bone. She is just as protective of Noelle as Beau is. I find it wonderful that Noelle has such a great friend in Shelby. She reminds me of my friend Ivy-Chanel back home in Georgia. I really miss her. Maybe, I can convince her to come visit me soon, I muse to myself.

"Shush!" Noelle says," her voice pulls me from my thoughts. "You need to calm down, Shelby. "And quiet down too," she adds. "We don't need to bring attention on ourselves. You never know when there is some trashy tabloid reporter lurking in a corner, just waiting to get a story and twist it to their way of thinking.

"You're right," Shelby instantly calms down. "I'm sorry," she adds.

I look between the two friends. I can see the deep affection and concern Shelby feels for Noelle. I wonder if Noelle's feelings holds any validity or if she's just being paranoid. I know being a new mother and being married to a rock star can take its toll on the best of us," I reason to myself.

"Okay! Enough about me and my paranoid ways. I still want to know how your family feels about you deciding to live and work in New York. I also want to know, how are you and Hunter doing?" Noelle asks me with a smile.

I feel all giddy inside, when I think of Hunter and the love we have for each other. I think of how my life changed…all because of my acceptance to his proposal.

"Look at her, Noelle. You see how dreamy her eyes get, when you bring up Hunter's name? Yeah, I do believe, our girl has it bad," Shelby says with a giggle.

"Uh-huh," Look, who's talking. I see the way you and Erick act together around each other. I be saying like…get a room, will you? The two of you acts like horny teenagers and can't keep your hands off of each other," I tease Shelby. But to answer Noelle's question, my family misses me terribly but they are happy, that I'm finding my way in the world. And I can't ask for a better man to love me than Hunter. I fall in love with him more and more each day," I add.

"Madison, is in love! She's glowing with it," Shelby teases.

"I have to agree," adds Noelle. Let's just admit, we all have it bad, when it comes to the men in our lives.

"Agreed!" Shelby and I say in unison. We pick up our glasses and toast to the obvious love and adoration, we have for the men in our lives.

CHAPTER 7

Victor

Noelle looks so beautiful in a pink body hugging dress and a pair of darker high heels to match. My dick hardens as I remember how it feels to be buried between her thighs in her moist heat.

She looks around the restaurant but a huge potted plant conceals me from her view. I can see Shelby's mouth running a mile a minute. I wonder what kind of nonsense she is spewing in Noelle's ear. Shelby is like a pesky fly, always buzzing around but hard to get rid of. There were plenty of times, she stuck to Noelle like glue, even during the times that I wanted to be with Noelle alone. I think of our college days, even if now those days seem like a dream.

"May I refill your drink sir?" The waitress asks, as she cuts into my thoughts.

"No," I'm fine for now," I reply, before giving her a dismissive glance.

"If there is anything you need, just let me know," continues the pesky waitress.

"If I want anything; I will be sure to let you know." "Now get gone bitch," I mutter under my breath. Damn, she's getting on my last nerve. All I want to do is to be left alone to watch my beautiful Noelle.

"Did you say something sir?" The waitress inquires.

I look at her and frown, before speaking. "There is nothing else I need. You may go," I ground out between clenched teeth.

I will bid my time and I know the perfect time will soon present itself, for me to my plans in motion.

I sit in the restaurant and continue to watch my sweet Noelle. She smiles easily as she converses with her friends. I don't know the new friend she and Shelby are having lunch with…but they seem to be having fun. I think back to the snowy night of when everything changed between Noelle and me forever. Those awful words have come back to haunt me and made her run into the arms of some punk rock stranger who don't deserve her. My eyes glaze over with memory as that nights takes over and replay itself like a movie reel in my mind.

I can hear Noelle's footsteps as I ran behind her on the sidewalk. She hurries to press the button on the wireless remote to open the doors to her sky-blue 2012 Honda Accord. The car lights automatically blink on as I gain on her. She looks back at me to see how close I am to catching up with her. I was shirtless as well as shoeless; but my long legs make quick work of the distance between her and me.

She quickly let herself inside the car, and the doors lock automatically behind her. I catch up with her by the time her door closes. I reach for the door handle anyway but she's locked the car doors. I hit the driver's side window with my fisted hand. I didn't pay attention to the pain that shoots through my hand and wrist from the impact. A loud thud sounds at her driver's side window from my continuously beating against it. I can tell I frighten her because she jumps in fright as she look up into my fury filled face filled with outright anger.

"Open the door, Noelle, and come back inside. It is too cold for you to be out here without a coat on. Are you trying to kill yourself?" I scream at her with anger in my voice.

"Look who's talking," she scream through her car window. "You are the one who is standing out there in the cold without a shirt on, or shoes for that matter," She wipe more tears from my eyes with the back of her hand.

I can tell she is hurt by my order for her to get an abortion after telling me she's pregnant. I can't tell her the real reason that I don't want another child. The real fact is that she doesn't even know I have another child. These thoughts bombard me as I try to get Noelle to come back to the apartment and out of the cold. Even in her anger, Noelle concerns herself with me standing out in the cold shoeless and shirtless in the cold, half-naked in nothing but a pair of loose fitting D'Marge jeans.

"Go back inside, Victor. I need some time to clear my head without you around," She yell loudly to get her point across.

"You are acting childish, Noelle, instead of acting like the twenty-five-year-old woman you are," I shout at her. I am more furious with myself for getting another woman pregnant. I love Noelle more than she will ever know but I have also fallen in love with the mother of my child. I have kept this secret for a while...maybe it's better if I let her go. I just can't see myself wanting another child right now. Especially since Samantha is demanding me to be with her and Victor Jr.

Noelle continues to glare angrily at me through the window before starting her car. "I am acting like a responsible woman. You are the one who is acting like a child. You don't want to man up to the situation that we both created together. How dare you ask me to get an abortion just because you aren't ready to become a father," She shout as fresh tears form and spill down her cheeks. "You don't have to worry about me and my baby. I will handle this situation from here on out. You can pack up your shit, or do whatever you want to do," She says before the sound of squealing wheels gave me no time to reply.

I look at Noelle drive out of my life that night. I stood out in the cold winter's night and watch the taillights of Noelle's car disappear from sight and out of my life.

The buzz of the lunch chatter in the restaurant pulls my thoughts back to the present moment. Noelle and her friends has left while I was in deep thought.

"Damn it!" I mutter aloud. A couple at a table across from me looks at me strange but I can care less. I think about how beautiful she looked on the day of her wedding. I should have broken up the wedding then but I hid from her sight like a coward. I have been keeping close tabs on her without her knowledge...

I ran Noelle straight into the arms of the rock star Beau Barringer. If I knew then what I know now, I would never ask her to abort my child. I haven't been the same since she ran away from me. If I can't have Noelle and my baby, then Beau Barringer can't either, I silently promise myself as I slip some bills from my wallet to leave on the table for my bill. Things will be looking up for me in due time...I begin to hum a tune under my breath as I leave the restaurant with a smile of satisfaction on my face.

CHAPTER 8

Noelle

"What's the special occasion, Beau?" I am stirring a pot of homemade spaghetti sauce in a pot on the stove when Beau walks into our beautifully designed kitchen with a dozen of red roses in his hand.

"Do I have to have a special occasion to give my beautiful wife roses?" He asks me, with a serious look in his eyes.

I stop what I am doing and turn the pot to simmer, before walking over to my husband with a teasing smile on my lips. "No, you don't need a special occasion to bring me flowers. I love any and all of your loving gestures," I say taking the roses from him and place them in a water filled crystal vase.

I place the crystal vase on the counter, before walking over to him face to face. "Thank you for the flowers, honey. They are truly beautiful." I say before placing my arms around his neck.

Beau automatically wraps his arms around my waist and looks deeply into my eyes. There is a crease between his brow, which lets me know he is overthinking or stressed about something.

"The roses doesn't come nowhere near as being as beautiful as you are, baby. I'm truly the luckiest man who walks the planet."

My cheeks become a deep hue of red from Beau's compliment. "Compliments like that will get you everywhere, kind sir," I tease him. "It will even get you an extra slice of the apple pie, I have baking in the oven."

Beau smirks, without taking his eyes from my face. "The pie does smells delicious, but I'd rather have you in place of the dessert."

My bikini briefs, becomes soaked, from Beau's declaration. Beau's face becomes a blur as his lips moves closer to mine. When Beau's lips meshes to mine, I become focused only on his kiss. His tongue slithers between my lips to mate intimately with my own.

I inhale his scent. His scent is like a powerful aphrodisiac to me. I shiver from the inside out as his hands begins to roam over my curves. His hands settles on my bottom and gives my ass cheeks a squeeze.

"Mmm," I moan into his mouth. He bites my bottom lip and sucks it into his mouth.

Beau arousal is felt prominently against my mid-section. "I need you, Noelle. Now." He grunts out against my lips.

"What about dinner? It will get cold, if we don't eat now…" I try to say but he cuts me off with another kiss. He slowly ends the kiss and looks deeply into my eyes. He sets my heart into a rapid beat from the intense heat radiating from his stormy blue eyes.

He turns and walks over to the stove and shuts off the burners, before walking back over to me. Beau didn't use words as his hands slid seductively down my body to the hem of my dress. He slowly lifted it up over my head before discarding it on the floor.

His eyes rakes over my body as I stand before him in nothing but my skimpy panty and matching bra set. He doesn't take the time to remove my bra but lifts it over my bountiful breast...This action leaves my breasts to spill out into his waiting hands.

Beau brings is lips against one sensitive hard nipple and begins to lick. My head falls back as the pleasure from his licking, courses straight to my slicken heat. My moans heats up the kitchen and my hands finds their way to Beau's electrifying black hair. My fingers rakes through his silken strands as he continues to feast off of my breasts.

"I love you more than anything in this world, Noelle," Beau mutters, before hooking one finger into my briefs. He slides down the offending material. I step out of the bikini briefs and leave them on the floor.

Beau wastes no time plunging two fingers into my moistness. I bite my bottom lip to keep from screaming my delight, so I let loose a delightful whimper instead.

"You do know that, don't you?" He asks in a thick emotion filled voice.

"I know," I whisper against his tempting lips. I stroke the side of his close cropped bearded jawline with my fingertips.

Beau turns his head and captures my fingers with his lips, before drawing them into his mouth. My wetness increases and leaks down my thighs. "Make love to me Beau," I croon out in soprano.

Beau, lifts me onto the center aisle counter-top, in the middle of our kitchen. He lifts me easily as if I hardly with anything at all. He takes one hand to release the belt around his waist. He unzips his slacks and let them drop to his ankles. He does the same for his black silky briefs.

My husband's hardness, springs forward, large and bold in all its perfections. "Pull your knees up to your chest," he orders me.

I love when my husband demands things of me sexually. It turns me on and I have no qualms of disobeying him. I know he only have my pleasure in mind. My ass cheeks are almost hanging off the counter-top. But Beau has me in the clutches of his hands. I trust him explicitly to not let me fall.

"Open your legs wider," Beau says with a guttural growl. His eyes are on my glistening pussy lips. "You have such a beautiful pussy," he continues in a sexual energized voice.

Beau, lifts my ass a little more and it hovers over the counter top. My hands slides up his chest before settling onto his shoulders for support. Thank God for Beau's height, I think to myself. His height, allows his shaft to be in the perfect position to slide into my wetness. "Oh!" I cry out, when Beau propels himself into my heated core, to embed deeply into my pulsating walls.

"Does this feel good to you baby?" Beau asks, as he pulls out his hardness from my glistening heat, before plunging back into me with a twist of his hips.

"Oh my God, yes!" I reply with a sensuous moan.

"How about this?" Beau asks, at the same time he splays my legs over his shoulders. This causes me to lie on my back on the counter top, but gives Beau deeper penetration into my core. His dick is throbbing as he deep strokes into me again and again.

He is the driver as he pulls my hips back and forth to match his rhythm. I am one blessed woman to be on the receiving in of so much undeniable pleasure, as he slides home into my waxed snatch, with intense deep strokes.

Beaus gyrations speeds up and so does the wetness that leaks onto the counter top, from my wet pussy.

"Damn, it, Noelle! You have some fucking good pussy," Beau grunts out as if he's in pain. "Mine. All of you belong to me," he says over and over.

My pussy takes that moment to contract and squeeze the hell out Beau's shaft.

"Arrgh!" Beau grunts out.

"I'm cumming, Beau," I whimper.

"Cum on baby…I'm cumming with you," Beau declares.

The world as I know it, falls away into nothingness. All that is left is Bea and I in a universe of our own, as his hot seed splashes against my walls. He blesses me with his essence to mix with my own.

The love between us, co-exists to gigantic proportions as we love on each other, the food I prepared earlier, is long forgotten.

***

Beau

"Good morning sleepy head," I say, kissing Noelle awake. Brandon, coo's as he lie between Noelle and me. Noelle slowly opens her eyes and looks down at Brandon, before turning her beautiful brown eyed stare to me.

"Good morning," she says with a smile.

"Did you sleep well last night?" I ask her with a smirk, because I already know the answer.

"Of course I did. I barely remember getting in the shower and getting in bed, last night, she admits.

"That's because I carried you upstairs and I had to practically bathe you, before putting you in the bed," I say with a chuckle.

"Beau Barringer, are you saying that I was so drunk from your lovemaking, that I didn't have any energy left to make it up these stairs, let alone to take a shower?" I ask him with indignation in my voice.

"Noelle Winters Barringer, that's exactly what I'm telling you," I respond with a chuckle.

Brandon takes that moment to out a wail.

"See, what you've done. Brandon wants you to stop picking on his mom," Noelle says before placing a kiss on Brandon's chubby cheek. "Are you hungry?" Noelle, talks to the baby.

"No, he's not hungry. I just fed him before I brought him in here to wake you up. Brandon, takes that moment to let out a loud gas bubble. Noelle's and my eyes meet and we both laughs. "Time for a diaper change and then a nap for you little fellow," I say standing and lift the baby to my chest.

"You are such a great father, Beau," Noelle says.

"I love this little guy. He's part of you…therefore he's mine," I states.

Noelle looks at me and a frown creases her brow. "Beau...," she says, before I cut her off.

"Let me go change Brandon into a fresh diaper and put him down for a nap. I will be back soon, there is something that I need to talk to you about."

"You sound serious, should I worry?" She asks and sits up in the bed, with her back to the headboard. Her loose curls falls in disarray around her face...making her more beautiful to me than ever before.

"We'll talk about it when I return," I reply leaving out the room, holding the baby close to my heart.

"That didn't take long," Noelle says, when I return to our bedroom. She is still sitting up in bed, with the sheet up to her chest. I know beneath the sheet, she is as naked as the day, she was born. I feel a stirring beneath my loose fitting pajama bottoms but I dismiss urge my desire for her to deflate itself, because I really need to talk to her.

I walk over to the bed and sit beside her. I look into her beautiful eyes and take her hands into mine. I brush a kiss across both of her hands before I begin to speak. "Do you remember the meeting that I had with my manager and my producers, a couple of days ago?" I question her.

"Yes, I remember. What about it?" She asks, looking directly into my eyes.

"I have to go on tour in Europe, to promote my latest album," I reply.

"Oookay," she drawls out her reply slowly. "How long is this tour supposed to last?"

"One month tops," I say but cringe inside, when I have to answer her.

"A whole month!" She exclaims and tries to pull her hands from my grasp but I don't let her hands go. "Why are you just telling me this Beau? Why didn't you tell me the moment you found out about you having to dessert me and Brandon for so long?"

"I'm sorry," I say with a slump to my shoulders and a heaviness enters my heart. "If there is any way I can back out of my contract without backlash, I would but I can't. I must fulfill my obligation. My career is not only at stake but the members of my band is as well. It's their livelihood," I reply with a plea in my tone for her to understand.

Tears enters Noelle's eyes and it breaks my heart even more. "Please don't cry baby," I pull her into my arms. I can feel her shoulders trembling, against my chest. I hate that I have to leave her. She's my heart and my heart beats for only her.

Noelle pushes away from me and I peer into her glossy tear filled eyes. "What will I do without you for a whole month, Beau?" She asks me in a soft tone.

"You have Brandon. The little tyke will keep you on your toes. Then there is Shelby and your new found friend Madison...I'm sure they will be glad to keep you company. Hunter and my parent's promise's to keep an eye on you also," I assure her.

"It's not the same as having you around, Beau. Nobody in this whole entire world can ever replace you," she replies.

I breathe in deeply. There is one more bit of information, that I must tell her, before I lose my nerves. "There is another bit of information, I must inform you of...," my voice trails off as my words fails me.

"I'm listening. Whatever else you have to say, can't get worse than you being away from Brandon and me for a whole entire month. Can it?"

I blow my breath out in a rush. I didn't realize I was holding it in until this very moment. "Courtney Nicks, will be touring with me and the band, while we're in Europe," I spit out.

Noelle gives me a hard look. She doesn't say one word. She just glares at me with a hurtful expression fixed on her pretty face. Tears brims in her eyes and spills over. I reach out and attempt to wipe them away.

"Baby, I know what you are thinking and I can promise you that nothing is going to happen between Courtney Nicks and me. The last thing you need to worry about is me betraying you with her or any other woman for that matter," I try to reason with her.

Noelle sniffs aloud and use the back of her hand to wipe her tears away. "Don't say another word to me Beau. I don't want to talk or hear another word from you," she say before jumping from the bed and runs to the bathroom.

She leaves me with the vision of her straight back and well-rounded moon shape ass, before she slams the bathroom door behind her. I arise to follow her into the bathroom, to make her listen to what I have to say. But the door is locked and I can hear the sound of the shower start.

I decide to leave her in peace with her shower and go downstairs to start breakfast. Maybe she will listen to me and open up her heart to me once again...after a hearty breakfast and her temper cools down.

CHAPTER 9

Victor

Just look at Beau Barringer, he thinks he has the reporters eating out of his hands, I think to myself, as he gives an interview to the Rock and Roller magazine reporter. I give the television screen my full undivided attention, as the reporter Charmaine Myers continues to question the great Beau Barringer.

"Mr. Barringer, how do you feel about your upcoming tour in Europe?" Charmaine Myers questions.

"I'm filled with excitement and I'm pumped," answers Beau Barringer, before flashing his million dollar smile for the cameras to capture. The flashes from the cameras can be heard and seen on the screen.

"You may be smiling now, Mr. Rock star, but you won't be smiling for long," I say aloud as I sit alone in front of the television screen in my apartment.

"Mr. Barringer, can you tell us how does your beautiful wife, Noelle, feel about you going on this month long tour, with your ex-girlfriend, the beautiful and talented, Courtney Nicks?" The reporter asks.

An unreadable expression crosses Beau Barringer's face, before he recovers and flash his winning smile once again. But I don't miss it…something is amiss with him and Noelle. A smile alights my lips in a flash. Noelle isn't even by her husband's side, this also tells me something isn't as it should be in paradise, and I chuckle aloud with this revelation. I can't wait to see how the perfect Beau Barringer answers this question.

"My wife Noelle knows the importance of me fulfilling my commitments. She also knows that I am doing what I love and she wants the best for me and my career. She also knows that Courtney Nicks and I are just business and the tour in itself is a business of promoting my album," Beau says.

"Yeah, he's hiding something alright. My Noelle isn't happy with her hubby going away for so long. But that's alright, I will be here to take up his slack. He doesn't love her as much as he say he does, if he can be traveling all across Europe, with a woman he used to and maybe still does, fuck on the regular..." I say aloud as I have this conversation with myself.

"Wow! I must say, that you have a very understanding wife, Mr. Barringer. I know myself, if I were your wife, I would have some reservation about you going half way across the world for a whole entire month, with a woman you used to be in love with," The reporter replies as if trying to get a rise out of Beau.

I laugh even louder and clap my hands in glee from the antics of Charmaine Myers. "Damn, she's good with her line of questioning," I mutter aloud. I wish I can see the look on my Noelle's face, right at this moment, I think to myself. I know her expression alone will tell how she really feels.

"Noelle is one in a million. She's very understanding of my career. She knows that I love Noelle and she knows this...There isn't another woman that walks this earth, that's a threat to her or our marriage. I live and breathe my family. She and Brandon is my world. I need them in my life to survive and I will never do anything to break up our happy home." He ends the interview on a note of perfection.

"Aww, This is why you Beau Barringer of the wet drams of many women, young and old alike. We should all be so lucky to have a Beau Barringer in our lives," Charmaine Myers says as she smiles at the camera and wraps up the interview. "On behalf of all of us at Rock and Roller magazine, thank you for your time and thank you for gracing us with this interview," she flashes Beau a flirtatious smile.

"It is my pleasure, Ms. Myers," Beau returns respectfully.

"Back to you Bob," Charmaine turns over the rest of the show to her colleague.

I have heard enough, I click off the television screen with the remote. "Where the hell do Beau Barringer get off with calling Brandon his son? There is no mention of his real father, which is me.

Beau Barringer is in for one hell of a rude awakening and he doesn't even know it yet! Just as easily as he stole my woman and baby, he can have them stolen back. I will have the last laugh, I tell myself. I will have my woman and baby here with me…Here with me is where they belong. And Beau Barringer will be left out in the cold…No better, than he deserves.

CHAPTER 10
Noelle

"Noelle, you have to remember, that Beau is who he is and he needs to fulfill his obligations of his contract, sweetie. I know you will miss him and all but you have us. Isn't that right, Erick?" Shelby asks her boyfriend, when he walks into the room with us each a glass of ice tea.

"Of course we will be here for Noelle. Beau loves the ground you walk on Noelle and you shouldn't spend your last days, he has at home before the tour with you giving him the cold shoulder. You are breaking the poor man's heart," Erick sets my glass on the table on a coaster in front of me. "Give me this big boy," he reaches for Brandon to hold in his arms.

"Don't you be getting any ideas, honey," Shelby directs her words towards Erick. "No ring and marriage...no babies," she states.

Erick rears back his head to let out a hardy laugh. "All in good time my dear one. I wouldn't dare think of putting the carriage before the horse," he replies taking a seat on the sofa besides Shelby. "No offense towards you, Noelle," he says to me in afterthought.

"None taken, Erick. I love Brandon and thank the good lord for him every day, but I wish his real father was Beau," I admit truthfully.

"I wish that as well agrees Shelby. But it is what it is and this little guy, will be loved and suffer for nothing in this world, regardless of whose genes he carries," she says before leaning down to place a kiss against Brandon's chubby cheek. "He smells so good," she sniffs him, under his soft neck. "I can just eat him up," she then takes the baby from Erick, to hold him close to her bosom.

"Wait a minute, I wasn't through having my bonding moment with the baby," Erick says, with a frown on his face.

"You two are so silly but you two better stop spoiling him or I will be calling you over at two thirty in the mornings, when Beau leaves.

"I will come running. He's my god son after all," replies Shelby.

"You hear her, Erick. You will be my witness, whenever I call Shelby and she complains about getting up that time of the morning, right?" I tease.

"I will definitely be your witness," replies Erick with a twinkle in his eyes.

Whatever, will I do without the two of you?" I ask them feeling sentimental all of a sudden.

"Aww, sweetie, you will never have to find out. We will be two old women, gum less and eating applesauce and I will be your ride or die chick," says Shelby.

Erick bursts out laughing from Shelby's declaration. "This woman here is something else," he says between chuckles.

"That's not funny!" Shelby swats Erick against his shoulder with her free hand. She mean mugs him, then burst into laughter of her own.

"You two definitely needs to get married and have a little one of your own. You two are going to make the best parents," I say with a smile, before my cell phone starts to vibrate loudly from my purse.

"I bet that's Beau calling you," says Shelby.

"I doubt it. Beau and his band are in the studio tonight. Courtney Nicks, flew in last night," I reveal before reaching into my clutch, for my cell phone.

I frown, when I notice an unknown number on display. I decide to answer it anyway. "Hello," I speak hesitantly into the receiver.

"Hi Noelle, its Victor," the caller says.

"I know your voice Victor," I say before looking at Shelby and Erick. They are looking at me with surprise in their eyes. "What do you want Victor?" I hadn't yet forgiven him for the scene he caused in the hospital all those weeks ago.

"I need to see you," he wastes no time in saying.

"No, I don't think that's a good idea. Whatever you need to say, we can say over the telephone or not at all," I can feel myself getting miffed.

"I got the papers that Beau sent over by courier," he reveals.

"What papers, Victor? I absolutely have no idea, what you're speaking of."

"Oh, really? I find that very hard to believe, Noelle. I have paternity papers from your Rock star's lawyer, urging me to sign over my rights to him. He wants to give our son, the Barringer name. I'm very disappointed in you Noelle. How can you go behind my back and lawyer up against me with your husband?" Victor spits out in an angry voice.

"I didn't know Beau had paternity papers drawn up," I reply in surprise. Whether Victor believes me or not is his call but I am telling him the truth.

"What does Victor want, Noelle? Is he harassing you?" She asks me with a frown on her pretty face.

I hold up my hand at her to get her to calm down. Lord, knows, that I don't need shit to escalate by getting Shelby involved in this conversation. She will only make things worse, I am sure. There is hardly any love lost between her and Victor as it stands.

Shelby gives me an eye roll before she whispers something to Erick. Erick looks down at Shelby and shakes his head in the negative. Shelby says something else but I can't make out her words, because Victor is going on and own in my ear, about how I have wronged him.

I sigh inwardly before expelling my breath from my lungs. "Victor, have you forgotten the reason that I'm married to another man and why another man is raising our son? You wanted no part of our baby…therefore you wanted no part of me. Besides, don't you have your hands full with the son you have by Sammy or Samantha something or the other?" I inquire.

"The bitch went back to her husband!" He chokes out.

"Well, I can't say I'm surprised by that fact," I admit. "But you can still be a father to the child you want," I urge him. I urge him towards his other son, in hopes he will leave Brandon to me and my husband to raise as we see fit.

"The bitch and her husband took Victor Jr. away. She followed her husband to Japan, after he received a promotion to start up a new company over there. Can you believe that shit?" He asks. His voice gets louder with each word he utters.

"Victor, why did you call me from an unknown number?" I cut in to ask him, to slow him down from his vindictive words about Samantha.

"I have a new phone. I guess it has something to do with my new cell phone company," he stutters out.

I can feel he is lying but decide not to call him on it, since it really doesn't matter to me in one way or another. "Are you going to sign the paternity papers that Beau lawyer sent over to you, Victor?" I decide to ask him.

"Do you want me to sign them, Noelle?" Victor asks in a too calm of tone to his earlier erratic uncontrollable tone of voice.

"Yes, I want you to sign them. You promise me once that you would. Remember?" I ask him.

"I need to talk to you face to face about this Noelle and I need to meet my son...at least once, before I make a life altering decision like this. Have dinner with me and we will discuss it then." He replies.

"I don't know, Victor…" My voice trails off, as I can feel myself wavering. Maybe if I see him face to face, I will be able to convince him to do the right thing," I convince myself.

"If after we talk and you don't want anything else to do with me, I promise you that I will sign the paternity papers, without bothering you ever again," Victor says in a sincere sounding voice. "I'm truly sorry about my actions in the hospital that day too, he adds.

Victor last words are the deciding factor in me meeting with him. Victor still has decency in him and will do the right thing for me and my family…I am sure of it, I try to convince myself. Beau will be furious if I meet with Victor but he will be leaving for his tour in a couple of days. When he leaves, I will meet with Victor. When he returns from his tour, the papers will be signed and he will legally be Brandon's father in every way…including name.

"Text me your phone number and I will be in touch," I say to him before ending the call without giving him time to reply.

"What does Victor want?" Shelby wastes no time in asking, before my call is fully disconnected.

I'm going to get Victor to sign over his paternity rights to me and Beau. I think he's finally realizes, it's in everyone's best interest for him to do so," I reply.

"Don't be naive Noelle. Victor is only playing on your sensitive good nature, but I see right through him. He promised to sign papers relinquishing his rights last winter, remember?" Shelby asks.

"People change Noelle. I believe it's possible that Victor has seen the light and error of his ways. He's paying for it by Samantha, leaving him high and dry. She went back to her husband and they've moved to Japan," I reveal.

"Finally, karma has begun to work," cuts in Erick. "He deserves every bad thing that karma has to offer in his treatment of you. I still feel like going over there to kick his ass. What the hell was he thinking?" Erick asks as he shakes his head from sad to side.

"I agree," Shelby put in her two cents. "You don't owe Victor a thing Noelle. From your conversation, I understand Beau has his lawyers working on Victor. Let Beau's lawyers do their jobs. Stay far and away from Victor, I don't trust him, one tiny bit," she adds.

"You're right," I quickly agree with Shelby. I will just keep my plans of meeting with Victor quiet for now. Shelby will only try to talk me out of it and Erick will possibly tell Beau. I won't even mention to Beau about learning of his plans about having paternity papers drawn up, without informing me. In doing so, I will have to tell him how I found out. So, I will just have to keep it to myself. Besides, I'm a grown woman who is capable of handling Victor. I will handle Victor in my way and all will be right in Beau's and my world afterwards. This I'm sure of, I tell myself before changing the subject of Victor and enjoy the rest of my visit with my friends.

CHAPTER 11
Beau

Noelle looks beautiful in her textured lace blouse and a paisley print skirt that flirts above her knees. Her legs are left bare to my view. Her feet are encased in a pair of colorful sandals to match the bright lively colors in her print skirt.

"You were quiet on our ride over. Are you sure you feel up to having dinner with my family tonight? We can turn around and go back home if you like," I say to her as Charles pulls up to the front of my parent's large home, which looks more like a castle from the outside and inside alike.

"We're here now," she says with a quiet reserved voice. Her beautiful eyes reflects the sadness that resides within.

"May I have my old Noelle back? I miss your beautiful smile and the light that reflects from your eyes. I need her back on my last night here before I leave for my tour on tomorrow. Please," I beg of her.

Noelle lets out a long sigh, before she turns to me with watery eyes. "I can't help the way that I feel. We have been together and never apart for more than a week at a time, since we've been married. I didn't go back to work, after my six weeks were up because you asked me to. Now, I regret that decision, because at least I would have my job while you're away."

"Brandon is so young. He needs his mommy home. But if you're not happy by the time I return, we can hire a nanny and you can go back to work. I don't want you to, but I will leave the decision up to you," I say to her.

"It's not so much about me going back to work…it's really about how much I'm going to miss you," she admits truthfully.

"I'm going to miss you too, baby. Hell! I miss you already when I think about not waking up and seeing your beautiful face in the mornings," I admit.

Noelle sniffs loudly, Charles and my eyes meets through the rearview mirror. He gives me a look of sympathy before he hit a button on the console to raise the partition between us to give Noelle and me some much needed privacy. Brandon is asleep and strapped down in his carrier facing us on the seat across from us.

I remove my seatbelt before doing the same to Noelle's. I pull her unceremoniously onto my lap and bring her head against my chest, before cradling her in my arms as if she is a small child.

"I realize, I've spoilt you with my undivided attention for all of these months," I try to let my voice be light but I fought like hell to hold my own emotions under control. I must remain strong for the both of us, I tell myself.

"

"Don't tease me Beau. Nothing is funny about you leaving us," Noelle mummers against my chest, where her head is buried.

I expend a deep breath, before placing a kiss atop her fragrant fluffy curls. "I know it's not funny sweetheart but you don't want to see a grown man bawl his eyes out, do you?" I ask her in a serious tone of voice.

She pulls away from my chest, to search my eyes deeply before she speaks. "You better not be locking lips with Courtney Nicks again, while you're away. I want so easily forgive you next time, if ever," she warns me.

"These lips are yours. I promise!"

"They better be or there will be…," Noelle's voice trails off as a loud rapt on the limousine's back window startles the both of us, including Brandon, who lets out a wail for someone disturbing his sleep.

Noelle slides from my lap. I reluctantly let her go to soothe the baby. I open the limo's door and come face to face with my brother Hunter and Madison right by his side.

"What are you two doing in here, instead of coming inside?" Hunter asks, with an easy grin on his face.

"None of your business," I tell him with a smirk, before getting out the vehicle first and then helping Noelle out with the baby as well.

"Hello Beau and Noelle," Madison says, before making a beeline for the baby.

Hunter looks at me and shakes his head. "It seems when my nephew is around, no other man gets any attention," he says with feign hurt in his voice.

"He's so sweet!" Madison says and relieves Noelle of the baby carrier. "He deserves everyone's attention," she adds walking off into the house, which leaves everyone else to bring up the rear.

Billy Barringer holds us all in his spell as he tells Noelle and Madison about the antics that Hunter and I got into when we were little boys. Between bites of the grilled spicy salmon, served over a bed of fluffy rice with a quinoa salad, drizzled with a tangy vinaigrette on the side...Laughter can be heard in great supply around the dining room table.

Bethany, keeps our wine glasses replenish as we drink of the fruity wine that goes exceptionally well with our meal.

"Who wants dessert?" Inquires Emma Barringer, my mother as she looks around her full table with delight in her eyes.

"I do," reply me and Hunter together.

"I knew you two were going to be the first one to speak," laughs our mother. "Bethany, you may bring dessert out now," she instructs the maid.

"Yes mam, Mrs. Barringer," Bethany replies with a friendly smile, and goes off to the kitchen to bring in the dessert that the cook prepared for our evening meal.

"Madison, how are you fitting in at the company? I'm hearing nothing but good things about you," my father says with a grudging admiration, for Madison.

"I'm fitting in very well. Everyone in the office is very friendly and doesn't hesitate to answer any questions, I may have from time to time," she replies with an enthusiastic tone of voice.

"Good…good," my father's voice booms out.

"Have you and Noelle heard from that lunatic of an ex-boyfriend of hers lately?" My father directs his stare between Noelle and me.

"No sir, we haven't heard from him. I look over at Noelle and she gets this funny look on her face. She looks at me and then quickly looks away. I wonder what that look is all about? I will have to ask her about it later, when we return home.

"You must not be a stranger, while Beau is away Noelle. Billy and I want to see lots of you and Brandon. I have a positively excellent idea," mother says, and a sparkle enters her eyes.

"Here goes Emma and another of her bright ideas. What does this idea entails, Emma?" My father asks with a chuckle.

"Oh, hush, Billy!" Mother says in her excitement. "I think it will be a grand idea, if Noelle and Brandon moves in with us, while Beau will be away on his tour. She won't have to be in that big house by herself," she adds.

"I think that's a wonderful idea. What do you think sweetheart?" I ask Noelle.

"Thank you mother Barringer, but I won't be totally alone. I have Brandon to keep me company. And I can't dare impose on you and father Barringer," she replies.

"You won't be imposing," Hunter chimes in. "Mother will love having you and Brandon here. You know she's fallen in love with Brandon and you will be doing her a favor by moving in this big mausoleum of a house," he says with a laugh.

"Hunter!" Mother admonishes him for calling her home a mausoleum.

"I'm only teasing mother. I love it here, even though I have my own place now. This will always be home to me," Hunter adds to pacify our mother.

Our mother beams at Hunter as she looks adoringly on her youngest son. "Well, just give my offer some thought Noelle, before you make up your mind for sure," she begs.

"Thank you and I will let you know, if I decide to take you up on your offer," Noelle replies.

"Leave the girl alone, Billy cuts in when his wife tries to speak again. "She already knows that she is welcome here at any time," he says before changing the subject to one of business.

I can hear Noelle let out a sigh beside me. It's as if she's glad the topic has moved on to other things, besides mother convincing her to move in with them while I am away.

I feel an uneasiness slip inside my spirit but I put it on my having to be away from my family. I decide to enjoy this night and not borrow trouble where it isn't any as we finish up dessert and head home.

***

Noelle

Beau comes up behind me, once we enter the bedroom. "You're still my tempting winter angel, in the midst of summer," he mutters, brushing his lips against my own.

I begin to shiver all over. Beau's intoxicating scent fills my nostrils. I inhale him, to remember his smell and hold the memory of this night, deep inside my soul. Beau, smooth my soft curls, away from my face. He peppers soft kisses all over my face, before once again capturing my thick lips into another favorable, soul stirring kiss.

I crave the touch of my husband. I want to feel his hands and lips over my entire body. "Beau, I need you so bad right now. Make love to me," I beg of him.

Beau pulls away from my clinging lips. A string of our saliva, hangs in the balance between us. Beau licks his lips…allowing our saliva to mix and mingle. He slowly undress me, before discarding his own clothing.

I allow my eyes to travel over his tan muscle bound body from head to toe. My eyes settles on his rigid hardness. His shaft throbs and pulsates, right before my desirous eyes. Beau drops to his knees before my heated flesh. No words are spoken as he nudges my thighs apart, before burying his face in my moist fragrant arousal filled flesh.

"Mmm," I moan in delightful pleasure, when I feel the first touch of his tongue against my slick nub. My knees go weak from the electrical shocks shooting through me.

Beau is loving me slowly and he's loving me well. I gasp aloud, when his hot tongue, plunges deep into my wet core. Beau's tantalizing talented tongue is sending me on an amazing high. A high, I never want to come down from.

"You like that baby," his voice vibrates against my plump hairless pussy lips. I groan aloud, when the vibration from his voice, shoots straight to my core.

"Yes! I love what you're doing to me. I always love what you do to me," I admit as a deep shiver overtake my body.

"Cum for me," Beau orders.

My hands entangle themselves into his electrifying dark strands. He attacks my pussy like a mad man as he buries his entire face into my pussy. I grind against his face as he eats me out with relish. I delight myself in the pleasure he is giving me.

"Give me your sweet honey," he mutters against my dripping puckered plump lips.

A keen moan arise from my throat and releases itself as I cum into his waiting mouth. He drinks of me…I fill his thirst to his satisfaction.

Beau stands and leads me towards the bed. I fall on the soft bed from his gentle push. The intense hot look in his stormy blue eyes, causes me to tremble. He hovers over my body for a moment and take in my naked body. He licks his lips before, he shift and his head swoops down to capture my lips once again.

I can taste my essence on his lips and tongue as he kisses me thoroughly. He uses his thigh to nudge my thighs apart and settle down between my thighs where I need and want him to be. The tip of his hardness enters me with excruciating slowness.

"More?" He questions me in a hot passion filled voice.

"Oh, yes!" I answer him on a whimper.

I groan, when he feed me another inch.

"How bad do you want it?" He teases me.

"Real bad," I wrap my legs around his trim waist, to prove my point...I contract my inner wall muscles around the tip of his dick.

Beau closes his eyes as if in torture. "Again," he bites out in a guttural voice.

"Give me more," I whisper softly.

Beau's eyes open at my demand. "You are a vixen," he says before I feel the sharp edge of his teeth, nipping at my bottom lip.

"Give me more," I demand of him.

Beau feeds me all of his inches as he embeds himself inside me to the hilt. "Ahhhh!" I gasp from the fullness I'm feeling. My inner walls muscles begin to contract around him once again. I want to put a choke hold on his dick, so he will remember the feel, for a long time to come.

"Damn, Noelle," Beau expels on a grunt. He begins to plunge into my heat filled damp flesh.

My hips begin to grind in compliment to his every thrust. His thrusting, turns into pounding as he beats my pussy into submission. A sheen of sweat begin to develop between our bodies. Slapping sounds can be heard throughout the bedroom as my husband takes me and bends me to his will.

I am compliant to the pleasure he gives me. He is more than acceptable to the pleasure, I give him in return. We are at one and peace with the universe...I don't know where he begins and I end. We are in sync and of one proportion...I meld into him and he melds into me. We are in a lover's paradise. I never want it to end…never!

"Cum for me, Noelle," Beau's voice penetrates my soul.

"Cum with me, Beau," My voice pierces his heart.

I feel Beau stiffen even more from my words. Soon, we both are falling…falling into a deep…deep abyss, as we cum together, as one being…expressing our beautiful love for each other.

CHAPTER 12

Noelle

I slowly come awake. I stretch my arms high above my head and slowly open my eyes. I can feel a smile blossoming my lips as I remember the night before. I can still feel the imprint of my husband deep inside me. Our essence is still sticky and gooey between my thighs.

I roll over to reach for him, but my hand come in contact with empty space. I come completely awake in an instant. The first thing I see is a red envelope and a lone red rose on the pillow where Beau had slept. I push myself up in bed and reach for the rose first. I bring it to my nose to inhale the sweet scent of the rose, before I sit it aside. I will put it in a vase later, I think to myself, before reaching for the envelope, which has a card inside. Beau's bold neat handwriting is scrawled inside the card.

"Sweetheart, you were sleeping so peacefully, that I didn't have the heart to wake you. I changed and fed Brandon before I left. I had a talk with him and made him promise me to let you get some extra sleep this morning. I know I wore you out last night, but I wanted to give you something to remember, until we reunite again. I love you dearly and we will talk or skype every night, or whenever possible. If by chance a day goes by and you don't hear from me, know that you are always in my thoughts and heart. You and Brandon mean the world to me...Because in truth, you and Brandon are my world.

Love always and forever,
Beau

I lie the card aside, alongside the lone rose. Tears slide down my eyes when I realize Beau has left without even awakening me. A sadness settles over my heart. I get out of bed and make my way to the shower. I adjust the temperature of the water before I step beneath the fortifying spray. I allow my salty tears to mix with the water. I allow myself my pity party for the duration of my shower, before pulling myself together for my son.

I step from the shower and dry off. I moisturize my entire body before sliding into my underwear and the rest of my clothing. I slide my feet into a pair of flats, before walking out of my bedroom to go into the nursery to check on Brandon.

I walk over to the baby bed to find Brandon's eyes open and alert. I swear he gives me the biggest toothless grin, when his eyes sees me. "Good morning, mama's sweet boy," I say softly to him. "You're such a good boy," I lean over the crib to pick him up and bring him close to my breast.

My heart feels with so much love for my darling innocent baby. His baby smell and softness, overwhelms me with so much warmth as I continue to hold his small body in my arms.

"Are you ready for your bath," I ask him, as if he understand every word that I am saying to him? I walk him over to the changing table and disrobe him of his cotton sleeper and soiled diaper, before walking over to the adjacent bathroom to get his bathwater ready.

Through the open doorway, I can see Brandon's brown eyed gaze tracking my every move. I walk back to him and lift him in my arms against a soft cotton towel, before placing him in his baby tub. I go through my morning ritual of bathing, moisturizing and powdering him down, before putting him on one of his cute little outfits. He looks so adorable, I think to myself. I'm glad he looks more like me than Victor. I hope it doesn't change in the future. I need no reminders who is the biological father of Brandon.

I frown as I make my way down the stairs. Victor still hadn't texted me his phone number like I asked him to. I wonder why, he hasn't since he's the one who wants to meet with me. Maybe I will go by his apartment later today and initiate the conversation of him signing the paternity papers, I muse to myself before I hear the sound of the doorbell.

I settle Brandon into his baby carrier before the sound of the speaker comes on. I press the button to answer the call from the private security guard. "Hi Seth," I speak into the intercom.

"Good morning, Mrs. Barringer," he reply in a respectful tone. "There is a Shelby Munroe, here to see you. Do you want me to allow her through?" He asks.

"Yes, please and thank you Seth," I say with a smile on my face.

"Guess what Brandon," I say aloud. "Your god mommy is on her way up. Isn't that great?"

Brandon looks at me and toots out his lips as if he didn't have a care in the world. I look at the monitor screen to see Shelby drive into the circular driveway. I lift Brandon and his carrier and walk towards the front door. Shelby is getting out her car by the time I open my front door.

"What bring you out this way this morning? Aren't you supposed to be working today?" I ask her.

"Of course I am but I'm playing hooky to spend the day with my best girl. Plus I come bearing breakfast," she says holding up the big brown paper bag in her hand. "Let's make a switch. I will take the baby and you go put our food onto some plates," she offer.

"This smells delicious," I say and make the switch.

"How's my precious baby doing?" Shelby talks to Brandon as she follows behind me on the way to the kitchen.

"I still can't believe you play hooky, just to spend the day with me and Brandon," I say to Shelby and place the food on two plates.

"What's not to believe?" She reply and place Brandon's carrier on the large breakfast nook area counter, so we can keep an eye on him, then she takes a seat of her own.

"I'm glad you're here," I say to her and slide her a plate. "What do you want to drink?" I ask her.

"Orange juice will be fine," she says digging into her plate. I give her a pointed look and she quickly bows her head and blesses her food. I do the same after getting our drinks and sitting down across from her.

Since I fed Brandon after his bath, he seems to be contented to nap in his carrier, while Shelby and I make small talk and eat our breakfast.

"I invited Madison to join us today. She said since she is a new employee at Barringer Estates, she didn't think it will be a good idea for her to play hooky. She's still trying to prove herself within the company. She doesn't want anyone to think she's taking advantage, because she's dating the CEO of the company.

"That's understandable," I say between bites of the delicious food. "You know how the office can be. Gossip, can and will spread like wildfire...whether it be true or not," I add.

"I agree," Shelby says and takes a sip from her glass of orange juice and peeps at me from under her long eye lashes.

"Why are you looking at me like that Shelby?"

"Like what?" She asks.

"You're looking at me like you have something on your mind."

"I wasn't going to say anything but I ran into Victor on the way over to your house. He was leaving this direction making a U-Turn, when I spotted him. He was in a different car...but I know his face anywhere.

"That's strange," I reply with a frown on my face. "I haven't heard a word from Victor since the day I visited you and Erick," I admit truthfully.

"Victor Wallace is a strange one and is getting stranger by the minute, Noelle. I really think he bear's watching. I can't forget the deranged look he had in his eyes, when he came to the hospital that day," She says with a visible shiver to her shoulders. "He's lucky that Beau didn't murder him with his bare hands," she adds.

"To be honest, I try to put that day far from my memory. Victor has apologized and I hope he means it, Shelby. He's never acted in the aggressive behavior, I saw in him that day. I don't think it will happen again," I say, trying to convince myself.

"You're much too trusting for your own good, Noelle. You have always been...You want to see the good in people, when there isn't any. Mark my words, there is no good left in Victor Wallace. When people show you who they are, you should believe them," she warns me.

I'm so glad I decided not to tell Shelby of my decision to meet with Victor. I am more determined than ever to get Victor to sign over his rights of my baby to me and Beau. I can't let this situation escalate any longer.

"What are you thinking about Noelle? You have this faraway look in your eyes."

"I'm just thinking about Beau and how much I'm going to miss him tonight," I reply, which is in part the truth. I didn't dare reveal my thoughts of Victor to her or she will be sure to thwart my plan.

"Lucky for you, I have an overnight bag in the car. I'm hoping you invite me over for a sleepover," she says with a giggle.

"Yes! I'm sorry I didn't think of it. We can order pizza and hot wings like we use to do in college," I reply with a big smile.

"We can stay up late watching scary movies too," Shelby adds. "Well, I can't stay up too late, because I do have to go to work in the morning," she says with a downward tug to her mouth.

"Our day and night will still be fun. We're hanging out like old times...that's what matters in the end," I say, feeling truly happy for the first time, after awakening to find Beau gone.

Shelby and I finishes our breakfast and plan our day. Brandon is asleep in his carrier the whole time...

CHAPTER 13

Beau

The music is blaring and I'm at my all-time best. Benji Rhames, my lead guitarist is vibing with my keyboardist, Keith Jones. My guitar adds a grating jarring note to our music ensemble.

I stand onstage in a black stretch style denim black jacket, with no shirt underneath and matching black jeans. The audience is going wild, when my voice join the music in a remake of a song, I wrote two years ago, titled, Wild Fire.

Wild Fire is a song of a raging love burning with the intensity of a wild fire. It's all consuming but becomes dangerous in the end. The crowd is loving this song. The Hot Pack Band is doing their thing in the accompaniment to stir the crowd and fans reaction.

My band, Courtney Nicks and I, have been practicing nonstop for two whole days, before tonight of our first appearance on stage here in Europe.

CHAPTER 14

Noelle

It's ten o'clock at night. I'm lying in bed with the remote control to the television in my hand, as I surf the channels. I am trying to catch a glimpse of my husband on the late news. That's the only way I can see or hear what's going on with him lately, it seems.

I haven't gotten a phone call from him in two whole days. I didn't sign up for this. Beau promised me to keep in touch but he's broken his word already. I miss him so much. I reach across the bed to grasp his pillow and bring it to my nose. I inhale the scent of his cologne. I doused his cologne on his pillowcase earlier, so it help me with sleeping alone at night. I may be selfish or spoilt but I want and need my husband home now.

My finger pauses on the remote button, when Beau's handsome face fills the television screen. He is at some premiere in London. Courtney Nicks is plastered to Beau's side like glue. A jealous rage fills my heart in an instant by the sight of the two.

"Why must you stand so close to my husband," I say aloud as if she can answer my question through the television screen. The show is live. I glance at my digital clock by my bedside. Its glaring red lights reveals it is now five minutes past ten p.m. It has to be five minutes past three in the morning there.

So this is what is keeping Beau too busy to call his wife, I muse silently to myself. I guess the saying holds true, when the cats the mice will play. Beau's smile is filled with sexiness and charisma as he smiles for the cameras. Courtney's boobs almost spills from her skin tight body fitting dress. I peer at the television screen through narrowed eyes.

"Oh my God!" I can see the dusky pink of her nipples peeking out of her dress," I say aloud in disgust.

Beau and Courtney waves to the crowd after signing some autographs, before getting in the sleek limousine together. The limousine pulls off and the camera flashes back to the enthusiastic overzealous faces of the crowd. The reporter ends her segment on a high note.

"As we can see the Rocker couple of this century are still endearing themselves in the hearts of fans and fanatics all over the world. After tonight's performances, you can see why the entire Nation dubs them the Sweetheart's couple of Rock and Roll! I'm Abigail Thomas for BBC News…Enjoy your morning," she adds and smile for the camera, before the station goes to a commercial break.

Angrily, I click off the television screen. I stare unseeingly at the black screen, before slinging the remote with fury across the room. "How dare Beau looks so happy and content with that woman on his arms? Did he lie to me, when he said the kiss he gave Courtney didn't mean anything, when he kissed her on stage, last winter? All of these questions and doubts war in my soul about Beau's commitment to me and our family, I silently think to myself.

I reach for my cell phone by my bedside. I have it charging but I unplug it and punch in a number for Beau, which is already on speed dial into my phone. His phone rings a couple of times, then goes directly to voicemail. I am beyond pissed and I wait impatiently for the prompt to leave him a message.

"Beau, I just saw you on the news, so I have no doubt that you are awake. I guess you rather spend your free time with your ex-girlfriend. You can be honest with me. If you are beginning to have feelings for her again, I think I should be the first to know, instead of reading about it in some magazine or waiting to hear about it on the news. I think I deserve more than that, don't you?" I can feel hot tears pricking my eyes, the more I talk. The beeper sounds off, alerting me that my message got cut off. I want to call back and finish my message but decide against it. It will only make me angrier, if my call goes to voicemail again.

CHAPTER 15
Beau

There is something different about tonight's performance. I am carefree and high on life. After the performance, I find myself indulging more liberally than I should in the great amount of alcohol that circulates around the room in plenteous supply. Even Benji, who is usually the watchdog is more carefree and relaxed, after tonight's performance.

"There is something I must do," I say aloud to no one in particular.

"What did you say, man?" Kendrick says in a loud voice, to make himself heard over the music.

"Hell, I don't know," I reply in a slurred voice.

Kendrick roars with laughter from my response. I join in with a chuckle or two of my own. "Let's drink to that," Kendrick picks up one of the many shot glasses lined up at our private table.

I pick up a shot glass and clink it against Kendrick's glass, then swallow the contents in one gulp. This last shot has taken me over my limit. I really need to get out of here to my suite and sleep this shit off, I tell myself. I attempt to stand but falls back in my seat.

"Damn Beau, when did you become such a lightweight? Look at the old married man, he can't hang anymore, Laney teases.

"I think you may have a point, that's why I'm getting out of here and letting you young folks have it." Even though Laney is older than me by a few years, I tease her back.

"Do you need help getting to your suite?" Benji asks.

"Nah, I'll be fine," I reply. "I'll see you all later and don't forget, we have a photo shoot for Time Out Magazine, in about nine hours," I inform them.

"We won't forget," they chorused.

I walk to the bank of elevators. I take the one which marks private. I use my pass key to open the elevator doors. A sweet fruity smell impales my nostrils. I look behind me and Courtney Nicks stands behind me. We haven't said too much to each other all night but now here she is.

"You're on your way up to your suite, Beau?" She asks.

"Yeah," I reply. "Where did you come from? I've hardly seen you all night."

"I've been around." She replies. "Look, there is something important, I need to talk with you about. Can we talk?"

"Court, can this wait to later. I really want to get up to my suite," I answer her.

"This won't take long, Beau. I promise you," she begs.

I don't say anything but I step back and motion for her to proceed me onto the private elevator. We ride up to my suite in silence. The elevator opens up into a clean spacious luxurious floor plan. The scenery from the top level picturesque window is breathtaking. It has a quaint view of the night's lights, alighting the city, which leaves one with a majestic view of the city.

In all of its awe inspiring beauty, all I can think of his falling into my bed, to sleep off the effects, of my overindulgence of alcoholic beverages tonight.

"Okay, talk," I direct Courtney over to a comfortable looking chair.

"May I have a drink of water first?" She asks.

I walk over to the bar, which has a fully stocked mini-fridge behind it. I open the refrigerator and retrieve her a bottle of water before walking over to give it to her.

"Thank you," she accepts the bottle of water. She untwists the cap and takes a small sip from the water bottle.

I cross my arms across my chest and wait for her to start talking. I don't want to be rude but I need to lie down before I fall down.

"Beau, do you remember how good we were together before our split?"

I look at Courtney and can honestly admit to myself that she is a beautiful and desirable woman. But I feel like I will place myself into deep shit if I have this conversation with her, right here, right now. "I don't think we should discuss the past, Courtney. We should leave the past in its rightful place," I reply.

"But Beau," she says and stand to her feet. Her jeans are so tight, they seem to be painted on her. The outline of her pussy lips can be seen clearly through her jeans, which indicates she has on absolutely no underwear. I don't notice the fit of her jeans on purpose but anyone with eyes will see the outline of her private area that is blatantly on display, for anyone to see.

"Courtney…," I attempt to cut her off.

She saunters over to stand face to face with me. Damn it! I curse to myself. Why did I let her come up? I know the trouble a situation like this can cause.

"I can tell you still want me, Beau. I can still feel the chemistry between you and me. Don't lie, because if you do, I will know it," she states.

"Courtney, you and I both know, I'm a happily married man. I love Noelle and I'm not going to do anything to hurt her," I remember my love for Noelle, even in my most intoxicated state of mind. But my little head seems to be having a mind of its own. The intoxicating smell of Courtney's perfume is getting to me. The way her lips glistens, brings back memories of those same glistening lips, wrapping around my hardness. I squeeze my eyes shut and take a deep breath, as I try to clear my head.

"Yes! I can see, you remember us together like I do. Your arousal says it all," she says before grabbing hold onto the length of my hardness. She gives it a mighty squeeze and jump nearly out of my skin from her electrically charge touch.

"I want you gone now!" I can feel myself getting angry and more aroused at the same damn time. Heat suffuses my entire body. I need to get away from her, fast and in a hurry. "I want you gone, by the time I come back from the bathroom," I order her. "Is that understood?"

She licks her lips sexily. I shiver inwardly but try to hold myself in check to not allow her to see her effect on me. I'm a married man, I continue to silently tell myself. I narrow my eyes at Courtney for her to see I mean business, before I turn on my booted encased feet and march off in the direction of the bathroom.

I stand at the bathroom sink. I reach for my cell phone that's attached at my waist. I want to phone home but notices my stupid battery has died. I lay my phone aside and turn on the cold water at the sink to wash my face to clear my head. I walk out the bathroom. The front room is empty. "Thank God, Courtney took my advice and left," I mutter under my breath and then walk out of the bathroom towards the direction to the suite's bedroom.

I flip on the light switch to flood the bedroom in light. The first thing I see is Courtney Nick's on the center of my king sized bed. She is as naked as the day she is born. I cannot lie. She is one beautiful sexy woman. Her hair lie splayed out across a pillow. I momentarily stand in one spot mesmerized, when she lifts her legs and her thighs falls open.

She reveals her wet pussy to my view. I'm finding it hard to swallow or even speak. She takes a finger and slide it inside her pink core. Courtney bites her lip and moan aloud. She watches me through eyes that are filled with lust. I can only hope my own eyes doesn't reflect the same lust; even though my cock presses against my zippered jeans, in a way that causes me to become uncomfortable.

"Beau," she sighs. "Come over and taste me. I know you want to," she moans out before sliding a sticky finger coated with her pussy juices into her mouth. "Mmm," she whines sexily. "Delicious! Come have a taste," she offers again.

I'm not going to lie. Courtney Nicks looks sexy as hell. Not even a year ago, I would have been tempted to dive into her deceitful web of pleasure. I would have been delighted to entertain her fiery heat between her thighs. But I have too much to lose. My Noelle is worth a thousand of Courtney's. My Noelle…my angel is my everlasting love who I dare not bring heartbreak to her existence…Not in my lifetime.

I walk over to the bed with purpose. I rip the coverlet from the bed and hold it up in front of me. "If you can't respect me and the only woman I love, then try having a little respect for your damn self! Regardless, you need to get the hell out of here. If you so much as try this again, I will do everything in my power to null and void the contract between you and me. I won't hesitate in letting the producers in on why, I want to terminate the contract," I tell her in no uncertain terms.

Courtney jumps from the bed and hurriedly throw on her clothes. There are tears sliding down her cheeks. My heart softens but I don't relent. The softening of my stance may confuse her, about my feelings for her and I don't her to misconstrue my intentions.

"I'm sorry, Beau," she says softly but is too ashamed to look me in my eyes. "This won't happen again…I promise you," she says before grabbing her clutch to run from the room. I can hear the elevator doors swish opens and closes, which lets me know she has finally left.

I fall back on the bed and breathe out a sigh of relief. I'm thankful for my resolve, to love my wife and only my wife. Things could have went much differently and I would have spent a lifetime living with regrets. I promise myself, that Noelle won't be hurt on my watch or by my hands. She and Brandon are my life and I won't do anything to destroy what we have built together.

CHAPTER 16

Noelle

I can't believe my eyes that stays glued to the television screen in front of me. I listen to the meteorologist as I feed Brandon his bottle of formula. He sucks greedily at the bottle as the meteorologist continues to talk of the developing storms that seems to be heading straight for my city.

"The hurricane is churning the east coast. It's destined for the mid-Atlantic. The cold front descends out of Canada nudges the Category three storm northwest. It's the perfect set up to ravage its way through New York City as well as all the surrounding areas."

"Oh my God, Brandon. I wish your daddy was here," I say aloud. I feel a foreboding tremble down my spine, as if someone is walking on my grave," I think to myself.

"New York Harbor has often sheltered the city's waning energy, from the violent gales that start at sea. The opposite is going to happen during this storm," the meteorologist reveals. "The way this system is set up, the usually moderate hurricane, has this scenario set up for a potential disaster. This will be the worst hurricane, in my predictions, that the city as well as all of the surrounding areas has ever seen. I must urge everyone to take precautions. Don't leave out of your homes, unless it's to get to a safer place. If you need supplies, now is the time to do so…Let me repeat, now is the time to do so," the weather man repeats.

My cell phone rings besides me. I give it a quick glance and notice its Beau calling. I answer the phone quickly, before putting it on speaker phone, so I can continue to feed Brandon his bottle.

"Sweetheart, I finally caught an uninterrupted moment of solitude, to call you. I'm glad I did, because I hear you all are in for a bit of terrible weather. I want you and Brandon to go to my mother's house. I won't worry about you there," Beau talks real fast before I can get a word in edgewise.

"I'm fine right here," I say stubbornly. I pull the almost empty bottle from a drowsy looking Brandon's mouth and lift him to my shoulder. I slowly rub his back gently until he lets out a loud burp.

"Don't be hard headed baby," Beau chides gently. "Pack up what you and Brandon needs for a couple of days and I will have Charles, drive you out there to my parents' home.

"No, don't bother Charles. I dismissed him while you are away. I'm used to driving myself around. I don't need Charles to drive me everywhere; I need to go."

"Honey, why are you being difficult. I'm not there to take care of you personally. Please let Charles chauffeur you and Brandon around," Beau begs.

"How is Courtney Nicks?" I steer our conversation in a totally different direction. "She must not be taking up your time right now, since you are just finding the time to call me," I say meanly.

Beau breathes heavily over the line. "What do you mean by that, Noelle?" He asks.

"I mean just what I said. Do I need to repeat myself verbatim?" I ask him.

"No, but, I'm trying to figure out where all of your animosity is coming from. I would think my beautiful wife will be happy to hear from me. Maybe I'm wrong," he injects a hurtful tone into his voice.

"I'm happy to hear from you Beau. I just wonder why you didn't answer my call the other night. I saw you and Courtney flouncing all over London together on the news; like you two were lovers. Yet you couldn't the find time to answer my phone call and check on your family back home," I say in an emotion filled tone of voice. I can feel tears build in my eyes. I squeeze them shut to keep them from spilling down my cheeks. But I lose the fight and the hot salty tears fall unheeded down my cheeks anyway.

"Baby, my phone died on me. I'm so sorry that I've been missing your calls. I want to call you more but I've been extremely busy and on the go. I swear to you...," his voice trails off.

"Beau, get a move on, it's time to go," I can hear Courtney Nicks voice call out to Beau in the background. I know her voice anywhere and it makes me sick to my stomach. I can see her and Beau locking lips clearly. The memory is still fresh in my mind as if it only happened yesterday.

"You better go. You don't want to keep your fans waiting for the perfect sweetheart couple of the century," I say in an angry jealous tone of voice. The green eyed monster is eating me alive and is succeeding in feeding off of my insecurities.

"Don't be like that Noelle. There is no need for you to be jealous of Courtney…Nothing is happening between us beside business and I can promise you that nothing ever will. You do trust me, right?" He asks in a hopeful voice.

His question is met with silence and more silence.

"Mr. Barringer," it's time to get a move on," an unfamiliar voice can be heard talking in the background.

"I love you Noelle and I love Brandon. You can trust in that…I have to go now. I don't want to but I have too. I will call you soon," he speaks hurriedly into the phone before hanging up. He didn't even hear me, when I said, I love you too…But all I am met with is dead silence.

CHAPTER 17
Victor

The hurricane winds are up to eighty five miles per hour and seem to be getting stronger by the minute. The days and weeks of my perfect planning has come to fruition. I've always known my patience would pay off and today is the day...I'm going to do what I have to do in the light of day and get away with it in plain sight.

It's nearing five o'clock when I pull my fed-ex truck up to the private gate entrance. I pull the bib of the navy FedEx cap low over my head, to shield my eyes and adjust the thick black rim frame glasses on the bridge of my prosthetic nose. My nose appears larger and has a bump at the bridge of the nose, as if it has been broken at some point in my life.

"Good evening sir, who are you here to deliver to?" The guard asks, looking at his clipboard.

"I'm here to deliver an important package to the Caudwell's," I reply, looking at my order sheet. I hold it up to the sliding glass window for him to inspect.

The guard frowns as he glance at his clipboard once again," before speaking. "It seems there has been some mistake. The Caudwell's are away and won't be back until sometime next week.

"Yes, my company knows this already. FedEx, has been instructed on where to leave this important package. If you will read the order form, you will see Mr. Caudwell's signature and the fax number, in which he faxed the orders of the package to be delivered."

The guard takes the order form and gives it deep scrutiny before pressing a button to allow me to drive through. "Thank you," I say, and accept the order form, he gives back to me, before driving through the black wrought iron twenty feet tall gate. "Damn that was too easy," I say aloud in the cab of the truck. "Stupid robo cop," I laugh aloud.

I follow the long circular drive on the printed out map of the estates of the rich and famous. I know the exact eight six hundred square feet home that belongs to the Barringer's. The impressive home is sitting on five acres of prime real estate. I guess Noelle has struck gold to be living the high life with the golden boy. I think to myself as I bring the truck to a complete stop, by the back entrance of their home.

I slide on my black leather gloves and grab my supplies before getting out of the truck. I need to work quickly and steadily. I find the direct power box and cut the lines to the monitors and alarms in one clean sweep. I know the generator will soon kick on for the lights but it will be no help for the alarm and monitoring system. The rain is starting and seems to be settling into a steady downpour with gusty winds at my back.

I work up a sweat by the time, I pry a side door open and walk into the house. It is quiet as I walk steadily but silently in my soft sole cushioned leather shoes, on the marble floor. I walk to the spiraling circular staircase. My steps are quick and swift as I make my way up the staircase.

On the second level of the home, I count five rooms but I can hear singing coming from a room at the end of the hall. I make my way to the open doorway. I can see Noelle bent over a baby's crib, singing gently to our baby. Lightning flashes through the window, the window making the soft glow from the lamp illuminate Noelle's well rounded plump ass to my view. I can feel a tightening of my crotch area as I admire her backside.

Noelle stands up from the crib and looks back but I quickly dart out of the open doorway and plaster myself against the wall. "Mommy will be back in a minute," she coo's to Brandon and walks towards the door. I am waiting and ready. She will never know what hits her...soon it will be over and she will be mine. Noelle and Brandon will belong to me. The way it's supposed to be from the very beginning.

Noelle steps out into the hallway. The chloroform soaked cloth in my hand raises...Noelle eyes widens and she gasps in fright. I waste no time in grabbing her with one hand around her waist and the other hand covers her mouth and nose with the chemical soaked cloth.

Noelle puts up a great struggle but she is no match for my strength. The chloroform takes much longer to work, than you see on the movies. Finally, her eyes closes and her body goes slack. I lift her nonresistant body easily in my arms.

I feel elation befall upon me. I feel in control…I feel like I am a god. I planned, I designed and I conquered. Beau Barringer will be left with nothing but a fancy house but I will have the prize. Let him feel the pain and burn in hell for trying to take what once belonged to me…

CHAPTER 18

Madison

"Hunter, it's getting worse out there." I pick up my cell phone and try to call Noelle again, because I am worried about her and the baby being all alone.

"I talked to Beau earlier today and he promised to talk her into going to our parents' home before the worst of the bad weather hits. Stop worrying, sweetie. I will call mother to see has she arrived," Hunter says before calling his mother.

I listen to the conversation that Hunter is having with his mother. He looks over at me and shakes his head no, and I begin to worry even more. I know I would be frighten to death if I have to endure this weather alone. I wait until Hunter ends the call with his mother before speaking.

"What did your mother say?" I ask him.

"She said they haven't seen or talked to Madison. She has called and was about to send a driver over to pick her up but I told her, I will go and check on her."

"We must convince her to come here, if she doesn't want to go to your parents' home," I insist.

"Before we go, let me check with one more person. She may be with Shelby."

"Great idea…I bet that whose she's with," Hunter replies.

I look through my list of contacts in my cell phone. I find Shelby's number and hit the call button.

"Hey girly, what's up?" Shelby answers the call in a cheerful tone of voice.

"Hunter and have been trying to get in touch with Noelle. We didn't like the idea of her being alone in that big house alone. Especially in this type of whether," I reveal.

"I just tried to call her myself but her call went straight to voicemail. Erick and I are on our way out the door to check on her now," she says.

"Great! Hunter and I are going over there as well. We will meet you two there. Between the four of us, we will convince her to come and be around her family."

Shelby agrees with my way of thinking, before we end the call.

"No luck, huh?" Hunter asks.

"Nope, Shelby hasn't heard from her either." I answer.

"Let's go," Hunter says. "Beau will have my hide if I don't look out for his precious cargo, while he's away." Hunter wastes no time ushering me out the door.

***

Hunter and I arrive about the same time as Erick and Shelby. They are just pulling in the driveway, when we arrive. We have no trouble of coming and going as we please, because we are on Noelle's and Beau's list of family.

We all greet one another and hunker down against the pelting wind and rain as we make our way to the front door. Shelby presses the doorbell and we wait. She presses it again, when we receive no answer. Hunter takes a look at the garage but the doors are down and we can't see inside.

"Maybe I should check around back," Erick suggests.

"I will go with you," Hunter says. "Keep ringing the doorbell, maybe she fell asleep or something," he adds.

"Okay, Shelby says. "But hurry up, this wind is going to blow little old me away."

I walk up to the door and test the door knob. It's locked up tight. I walk over and squeeze through a shrubbery and try to peep through a window but the draperies are closed.

"Hey!" Hunter and Erick comes running from around back of the house. The back door has been broken into. I called the police. Erick and I called out to Noelle but didn't get an answer," Hunter talks a mile a minute without catching a breath.

Erick rakes his hand worriedly through his wet hair. "I got a bad feeling about this," he says with a frown of worry on his face.

"Oh my God...Oh my God," Shelby says over and over again. She bends at the waist and starts to hyperventilate.

Erick rushes over to her and tries to talk her through getting her breath under control. I'm standing there speechless, with a stupefied look on my face. I can't believe this is happening.

"We should go in and check on Noelle and the baby. They may need our help," I finally find my voice to say.

"I should have come earlier," Shelby cries out loud. "I'm going in!" Shelby takes off at a sprint before anyone can stop her.

By the time we make it around back, Shelby is already running in the house, calling out to Noelle. We all run in behind Shelby and follow her up the stairs. She goes into Noelle and Beau's bedroom but we don't see any side of her.

We such room by room and even the nursery. There is no sign of Noelle or the baby. "Be careful and don't touch anything," Hunter warns in an emotion filled voice.

I can tell he is very upset, even though he tries to hide it. By the time we walk down the stairs, we can hear the sound of the police sirens.

"Noelle!!! Where are you?" Shelby screams and falls to her knees in the middle of the foyer on the floor, with fat tears streaking down her cheeks.

Erick goes over to Shelby and lifts her like a little rag doll in his arms. He holds her close and tries to comfort her as best he can.

There is a pounding at the front door. Hunter walks over with a slump to his shoulders to let them in. I stand there with a heavy heart as a shiver of foreboding floods through my body.

CHAPTER 19

Hunter

My parents arrive. The police has swept through the house and over the entire five acre property, since there has been a forced entry. There is no sign of Noelle or the baby. The police has the entire home dusted for fingerprints. We give them a sample of our fingerprints, in case we touched anything by accident, so ours will be excluded from the crime scene.

Although there is no sign of struggle, the police are still not taking any chances. They inform us that this will have to be kept out of the media until the next forty eight hours, as this is proper police procedure. They will try to get a handle on the case, while working around the clock, the lead investigator of the NYC department assure us.

I dread calling my brother but I know I need to be the one who does it. "I'll be right back," I whisper to Madison who is comforting Shelby, along with Erick by her side.

I look over at mother. Her eyes are bloodshot and red, riddled with tears of her own. Dad is sitting on the arm of the chair mother is sitting in with his arms around her shoulders.

I know it's a little after mid-night. Hopefully I can catch him between sets, if he's performing. I know he will never forgive me if I don't let him know what's going on. He won't give a damn about performing if his wife is missing.

The phone rings, then stops. The line is open…I can hear a cheering crowd and loud music. I can clearly hear the crowd chanting, *"We want Beau, we want Beau…we want Beau!"*

"Hello!" I say into the receiver. I can hear breathing on the other end but I get no reply. Then I hear a click, alerting me the call has ended or dropped.

"Did you reach Beau?" Ask Madison, walking up to me.

"No, but I will keep trying until I do. There will be hell to pay when Beau finds out his wife and son has gone missing."

"Son, the police might be keeping this under wraps, but we are the Barringer's and we don't sit around and twiddle our thumbs like little old ladies. I've just put in a call and hired a private investigator to look into this case for me. It's an old buddy of mine son that has his own private agency. You and Beau should know him. I think you all went to the same private school together when you were younger. His name is Asher Vallencourt."

"Yes, I remember Asher. I haven't seen him in ages though. I didn't even know he went into that line of work. I pray he's good, because not knowing where Noelle and Brandon are is driving me absolutely crazy," I admit, trying to hold my emotions at bay.

"I know son," my father grips my shoulder and give it a squeeze. "We are going to do all we can to bring Noelle and my grandbaby back home, where they belong. You just wait and see, we will find them," My father says in a reassuring voice but I can see the great concern in his eyes.

I look over at Madison and she has tears running down her cheeks. I open my arms to her and she walks into my embrace. I lay my head atop her straight black hair and close my eyes. I say a silent prayer that no harm comes to Noelle and my nephew. I pray are somewhere safe and sound and will be reunited with our family very soon.

"Did anyone reach Beau yet?" Asks Shelby stepping into the hallway with Erick by her side.

"I better go back in and check on your mom," my father says and walks off to go comfort my mother.

"No, I tried to reach him a little while ago. Someone answered the phone. I could hear breathing over the open line, before someone hung up on me," I reply.

"I don't think Beau would hang up on you, Hunter. That's strange," Shelby adds.

"Did you try and reach his manager Dave Dillinger?" Erick asks.

"I didn't think of that," I say shaking my head for my lack of common sense.

"While you try to reach his manager, I'm going to try and reach Beau...I'm going to keep calling and texting him, until something gives," says a determine Shelby before setting her plan in motion.

"I feel so useless," whispers Madison.

I look at her with understanding in my eyes. I feel the same way, I think to myself and place the call to Beau's manager.

Dave Dillinger's phone goes straight to voicemail. I hate to but I have no choice but to leave a message. "Dave, this is Hunter Barringer, Beau's brother. There is an emergency back home and he needs to call me as soon as you get this message. I must stress the urgency of him returning my call...You can reach me at this cell phone number. I don't care what time it is, he need to call me. It is of the utmost importance." I end the call after the voicemail beeps, letting me know the recording stops. "Damn!" I bite back a line of expletives that wants to force its way out of my mouth.

"Beau will call as soon as he gets your message," Madison, says caressing my back in a circular motion.

"No luck on my end either," Shelby hangs her head in defeat. "I left Beau a message, urging him to call one of us as soon as possible," she adds, in a sad tone of voice.

"Folks, my name is Troy Bryant, and I will be the lead investigator on this case. If each of you will be so kind as to give my partner her your names, your contact number and the relationship you are with Mrs. Barringer, someone or myself personally will be in touch with each of you. Does Mrs. Barringer's parent's live in this area?" Troy Bryant inquire.

Shelby is the first one to reply. "No, her father passed away some time ago, but her mother and step father, still lives in her hometown in Georgia. She is estranged from her mother, but I'm sure Madison can probably enlighten you how to contact them better than I can...since she's from their and know them.

"Do you happen to know their names?" He looks over towards me with questioning eyes.

"Yes, I do," I speak up. Her mother's name is Nichole and her step father's name is Terrance Roberts. I don't know their contact numbers but I can find out," I offer.

"I just need their names and the city of their resident. Thank you for the information, Ms. Powell, I think we can handle it from here," he says.

Investigator Troy's partner continues to take notes. "We will be in touch with all concerned," he adds. "Until then, we are taping this home off. The weather has gotten worst out there and I want to advise each of you to go home…wait on us to contact you and know we are on the case," he informs in a confident voice.

"Well, you heard the man," my father says walking into the room with my mother in tow. "Hunter, I think you and Madison should come with us and you two, should come as well," my father includes, Shelby and Erick in his offer."

"I think that's a great idea," I agree capturing Madison's hand in mine. "You two are coming right?" I ask Shelby and Erick."

"If you're sure, we won't be a problem," Shelby says looking at Erick for his approval.

"You two are close to Shelby, so that makes you our extended family too," my mother cuts into the conversation. "We won't take no for an answer. Besides, we have more than enough room and none of us need to be alone during this time of emergency," she adds in a sensible tone of voice.

"We accept," Erick answers for himself and Shelby.

"Let's get going then," My father directs all of us.

I take one last look back at my brother's and Noelle's home before taking my leave. I will Beau in everything that's within me, to call.

CHAPTER 20

Beau

"Dave, thanks for holding onto my cell phone, man. I thought I had it on silent. Good looking out!" I say walking up to him after our performance.

Just before going on stage, the ringer on my cell phone goes off. Dave offers to silent it since I was hyped and biting at the bit to perform. I thought no more about it and tossed it to him; so that I didn't waste precious time, to get on stage and start my performance, for the overzealous crowd.

Dave jumps as if I startle him, when my hand settles onto his shoulder. I look over his shoulder to see the screen of my cell phone is on the message screen. I don't have a lock on my cell phone, because I have nothing to hide. But for Dave to be sneaking through my messages isn't settling well within me.

"Beau! I was just...,"

"You were just what Dave," I snatch my phone from his hands as he looks at me with an expression of guilt written all over his face. "Why are you going through my messages, Dave?" The ringing of my cell stops me from questioning him.

I hope it is Noelle calling me. She is the first one I will call anyway, once I get to my suite, I think to myself. I look at the screen and I see it is Shelby number that appears on the screen, instead of Noelle. My heart at once becomes filled with concern, because Shelby hardly ever calls me, unless she can't get a hold of Noelle, for some reason or the other.

"Shelby, this is a surprise. What's up?" I ask her.

"What's up? That's the only damn thing you have to ask, Beau Barringer, what's up? Have you lost your fucking mind?" She screams so loud that I have to literally take the phone away from my ear.

"Calm down, Shelby. Why are you so upset?"

"If you would check your messages and texts, you would know, Hunter, me and your parent's have been trying to get a hold of you. Hinter even left a voicemail on your manager's phone, for you to call home, ASAP!" She is sounding more upset with each word that spews from her mouth.

"Let me speak to him Shelby," I can hear my brother in the background, speaking to Shelby.

"Beau, you really disappoint me," Shelby says before my brother voice comes over the line.

"Hunter, what's wrong with Shelby. She says everyone has been trying to get a hold of me."

"We have big brother," he sighs loudly into the phone. "Beau, you need to get home...like now," he says in a serious tone of voice.

"Little brother, I don't like the sound of your voice. Where is Noelle?" Is the first question, I feel compelled to ask.

"Beau, I hate like hell to tell you this over the telephone, but there's no other way to tell you this."

"Just spit it out!" I can feel a chill shoot straight down the center of my spine. "Never mind, just put Noelle on the phone, Hunter. I want to speak with my wife. Is she there with you?" I swallow the lump that's building in my throat.

"That's what I'm trying to tell you Beau. Noelle and baby Brandon have gone missing.

"What?!" I know I can't be hearing my brother right. I just can't be...

"What's wrong, Beau?" My manager looks at me with concern on his face.

I turn my back on him and put my ear back to my cell phone. "Please tell me that I didn't hear you right," I plead.

"Come home Beau. When your flight lands, come straight to our parent's. Your family will be waiting on you."

My heart is beating so hard and fast. It feels like it wants to jump straight through my chest. It feels like I can't take my breaths in fast enough. So I bend at my waist and try to catch my breath. My phone falls to the floor...I can still hear my mother talking but I am useless. It feels as if the world as I know is spinning out of control.

My spirit that soared only minutes earlier is now boiling in turmoil. Voices around me are calling my name. My ears mute them out...my eyes begin to burn and I squeeze them tightly shut. Hot water spills from my eyes, I don't fight it. I stand and whale out my sorrow into existence.

I don't hide my pain and turmoil. Laney grabs me and pull me into her skinny arms. I embrace her slim body, like she's my lifeline. I become weak at the knees but somehow, my skinny little drummer finds the strength to keep me from falling.

Kendrick and my other band members gather around me. I need to find the strength to move. I need to get home to Noelle and my baby. I have to find them…somehow I have too. Without the two most important people in my life, I want no parts of this world. I know this as truly as I'm struggling to breathe.

"We got you man," Benji's voice reaches my conscience. "What do you need us to do? We are here for you…all of us are," he speaks for them all.

"I gotta get home," my voice croaks out hoarsely. "Noelle and my baby is missing. I don't know all the details but I gotta get home now," I try to speak clearly over the lump in my throat but fails miserably.

"You can't just leave Beau, you have a contract to fulfill," Dave has the audacity to say.

"Fuck you and fuck the contract," I growl out with fury in my voice. "Is that all you care about? My wife and son are missing. I will give away everything I have right now if I can have them back with me. You do what you have to do and I'm going to do what I have to do for to find my family. Everything else doesn't matter," I say brushing past him to get as far away from him as possible. My hands are itching to throttle him on the spot, but I have other pressing matters to deal with. Like getting the jet ready for clearance to fly me home and back to claim my family. I will lean no stone unturned until Noelle and Brandon are back with me, where they belong.

CHAPTER 21

Victor

"Look how beautiful your mommy looks, while she's sleeping," I say to our baby, who is looking at me with what appears to be a curious expression, on his tiny brown face. I begin to hum to Brandon as I rock him in the rocker that I placed in this room a while ago.

Noelle is oblivious to her surroundings but I am filled with happiness to finally have, what rightfully belongs to me once again. It's a great feeling to know that no one, not even Beau Barringer, will be able to come between us ever again, I ponder to myself.

I always knew that my patience and proper planning would pay off in the end. I look down at Brandon. He is such a good baby. He hasn't made a fuss, until he's hungry or his diaper needs changing. I hope I put the diaper on correctly but if not, my love can rectify it once she awakens. I joyously muse to myself.

Noelle, begins to move on the large cot. Her curly long hair is half covering her beautiful face. Her eyes slowly begins to open and clashes with mine…There is a look of confusion, resting in her eyes. I smile but she slowly begin to frown. Her eyes glances at the small bundle in my arms. Confusion seems to flee her eyes in an instant as she become alert.

She sits up quickly on the bed. Maybe a little too quickly, for she grabs her head on both sides, with her hands. "Victor, what are you doing with my baby? Where are we?" She asks as she attempts to stand but falls back weakly on the bed, from her attempt.

"You may want to move more slowly," I warn her in a calm voice. "Why do you ask me such a question, about what I'm doing with our baby? I have a right to be holding our baby, don't you think?" I answer her with a question of my own.

Noelle sits upright on the cot once again. She takes my advice and move slower this time around. "Give me my baby, Victor," she says in a voice filled with panic. She stretches out her arms towards me as she reaches for the baby.

"He's fine where he is," I reply. "Brandon and I are having a bonding moment, of father and son. I think it's time for him to know the man who is responsible for his existence in this world; don't you agree, my love?"

"I'm not your love, Victor…Don't call me that and please give me my baby, please!" She continues to beg me, in an escalating pleading tone of voice.

"Don't you trust Brandon's own blood, to care for him, my love?" I ignore her request for me not to call her my love. I can't deny my love for her, when the source of her embodiment, burns through my heart like acid.

"Where are we, Victor?" Her arms fall down weakly to her sides. I notice she avoids my question. I decide to let it pass for now. But I have no doubt before long, she will be pledging her love for me once again, in the near future.

"You and Brandon are home where you belong. That's all you need to know for now."

"No!" Noelle says, shaking her head from side to side in denial. Brandon and my home is with my husband, Beau. I need Beau. Please let me call my husband," she begs as big tears leaks from her eyes.

Seeing tears leaking from her eyes angers me. I stand instantly and storm over to her. I can feel my temper becoming volatile and explosive. It doesn't take much to set me off lately. "Stop crying over that man! I despise the ground he walks on," I spit out.

Noelle cringes from my fury. Brandon starts to cry…I look down and realize that I am squeezing him much too tightly.

Noelle stands once again. "Give me my baby, Victor. You are hurting him." She reaches for out for Brandon…This time, I hand him over to her. I don't want to hurt our baby but its Noelle's fault for bringing up that bastard's name.

"Look what you made me do. Don't mention that man's name ever again, while you're in my presence." I march back and forth across the length of the room. "Do you understand?" I stop in front of her and look into her frightful eyes.

She holds Brandon protectively to her bosom. "I understand," she answers softly and sit back on the cot. She scoots back on the cot, until her back is to the wall. Tears continues to fall relentlessly down her reddened cheeks.

"It's good, that you finally understand. You and Brandon belong to me. There is nothing you can do to change that fact, so you better get used to it, if you know what's good for you. I know you must be hungry by now. I'll go to the kitchen and prepare you something to eat. Brandon formula and anything else you may need for him is over there in that pantry. I point towards the portable pantry. You can even warm his bottle in the bottle warmer," I inform her. Noelle doesn't say anything but watches me with a wary expression on her face. "I won't be long," I add, before walking over to the hidden door.

To the naked eye the door will appear like part of the wall. I press in a code from the palm sized remote, I pull from my pocket. The door slides silently open. I step through and close it effortlessly behind me.

***

Noelle

I slowly awaken. I have a whopper of a headache. I fight to open my eyes. When I first open my eyes, they are unfocused...I feel strange but don't know why. The last thing I remember is putting Brandon into his crib. Then everything went black, until this moment.

My eyes finally focuses on Victor...I see him rocking and humming to a small bundle he's holding in his arms. Awareness settles heavy on my shoulders, when I realize he has my innocent sweet little baby boy, in his arms.

I frown, as all of these unanswered questions, floods my mind. Where are we and how did we get here? Why is Victor holding my baby? I sit up on the bed and my head throbs. It hurts so much, I can feel myself become nauseated but I fight it and swallow the bile that arises in my throat. But I fight to speak through my uncomfortableness.

"Victor, what are you doing with my baby? Where are we?"

He looks at me with a crazed look in his eyes, before he answers me. Victor looks through me, instead of directly at me. I have never seen him look at me in this way in all the years; I have known him. The look frightens me…Victor frightens me. All I can think about is getting my baby from him. I am afraid for myself, but most of all, I am afraid for my innocent baby.

Victor's avoidance of my questions scares me to my bone. Please God, help my baby and me, I scream out my thoughts silently as I pray.

I almost pissed on myself when Victor becomes infuriated by my tears and the mention of Beau's name. His eyes went black and he squeezed my baby to his chest. He was like the devil himself, standing before me. Even in the presence of this evil presence, the safety of my baby is at the forefront of my mind. I had to get my baby from him or I would die trying.

"Give me my baby, Victor. You are hurting him," I stood and reached for my baby.

This time Victor hand my baby over, without me having to beg like before. He orders me to never mention Beau's name in his presence again. I knew in that instance that Victor is too far gone to be reached. He had lost all sanity to reason with. Oh! I wished I had believed Shelby. She was right...I was so far wrong in my thinking, to believe there was good in Victor.

Victor face goes from fury to calm, when he offers to go and prepare a meal for me. It's like looking at two men in one body. How had this big of change come over Victor, without me noticing it? I muse to myself as I take in my surroundings.

I scoot back on the cot with Brandon in my arms. The room is in all white, with beige undertones. I watch Victor walk towards the wall on the other side of the room. He removes a small black object from his pocket. He fiddles with it before the wall slides open. He steps through and the wall slides closed behind him.

If I hadn't been looking with my own eyes, I wouldn't believe it. There isn't any indication that a door is where the wall slid open. A heaviness fills my heart. I hold a whimpering Brandon closer to my chest. He cries and I cry, for I feel so alone. I wish for Beau or anybody to come and save us...To save us from Victor, the evil warden that imprisons me and my baby in these prison walls.

CHAPTER 22

Beau

"Beau, my darling son," mother jets into my arms as soon as I walk in the door. It has been over thirty six hours since Noelle and Brandon has gone missing. I have been existing on nothing but fumes, ever since I left London.

I catch my mother in my embrace. I bury my face against her shoulder. I feel lost and desolate without my Noelle and baby boy. "I went to my house before coming here but the police wouldn't let me in," I murmur aloud as my mother continue to hold me in her comfortably familiar arms.

"I told you to come straight here brother," Hunter says entering the room with Noelle following closely at his side.

I look at my brother with a solemn expression on my face. I pull myself from my mother's embrace. "Has the police thought to contact Noelle's mother?" I ask. It's strange that I am just thinking of contacting her mother. In all fairness, I know nothing about the woman, but her name. Even though Noelle hasn't seen her mother in years, she is still her mother and she needs to be here for her only daughter, I think to myself.

"Yes, Investigator Troy Bryant, said he would get in touch with her parent's," answers Madison. She is looking at me with worry in her brown eyes.

"It's my fault that Noelle and Brandon are missing. I should have been home to protect them." I can feel my gut twisting in knots as my heart beats erratically against my chest.

"That is so untrue, Beau. You are not at fault for their disappearance," Madison says before giving me a hug.

"You must eat Beau. You don't want to become sick…you must keep up your strength, for when Noelle returns to you," mother chides with a worried frown on her face.

All I crave for is for Noelle to be in my arms. She is all I can think about…Without her and Brandon, I feel so empty inside…I feel like I am existing but not a part of this world.

"Come into the kitchen Beau," I will have the cook prepare you something to eat. Then your father wants to see you in his study. You and Hunter both," she adds.

"I'm not hungry, so I matter as well go see what father wants now," I finally reply.

"When is the last time you ate something, Beau?"

I stop walking and turn towards my mother with a blank look on my face. "To be honest, I can't remember the last time I've ate," I reply truthfully.

"I tell you what, allow me to whip you up a quick omelet," Madison says as she come forward to hook her arm in mine. "It won't take but a jiffy, then you will be in the right mind to meet with your father."

I can see Hunter mouth a quick thank you to Madison as she leads me towards the kitchen. Even though I don't have much of an appetite, it doesn't take long for me to wolf down the omelet that Madison has prepared for me.

"Thank you for the food," I say to her. I stand and place a kiss against her cheek. "My brother is a very lucky man and I'm happy you're in his life." My voice catches in my throat, when I think of my winter angel Noelle.

"Noelle and Brandon will be found soon, Beau. You have to have faith. Faith, will see you through," Madison says giving my hand a reassuring squeeze.

"I hope you're right," I reply, before walking out of the kitchen towards the study to meet with my father.

I enter the study area to see Hunter, my father and a vaguely familiar looking man in deep discussion. They stop talking and look at me. After a moment, my father rises and walks towards me. He says nothing at first, but pulls me into a bear of a hug, before releasing me.

"Son, I'm glad you made it home in one piece.

"I won't be whole again until Noelle and Brandon are home in one piece, with me, where they belong" I reply. Each time I say Noelle's name, another piece of my heart chips away.

"They will be son…If I have anything to do with it. Your family, will soon be back with you in no time. That's why I need to talk with you. Do you remember, Asher Vallencourt?" My father asks, as we walk to his desk.

The familiar gentleman stands from where he is seated. He extends his hand in greeting. "Beau Barringer, it has been some years since I've saw you," Asher says.

Remembrance dawns, when I take in the full view of Asher's Vallencourt's face. "Yes, I remember you. It has been a long time," I agree. "But why are you here?" I question. I look from my father and my brother, then back to Asher and await an answer.

"Have a seat," my father orders and become the man in charge once again. We take a seat and face my father behind the big mahogany desk. "Asher is a private investigator. He is one of the best in the business and owns his own private investigating firms in the city. He only hires the best employees, such as ex-marines, navy seals and the like," my father continues. "Asher has agreed to take on our case himself as a special favor to me and our family."

I look over at Asher. "I didn't know you were in this line of work. Do you think you can find Noelle and my son," I ask him directly. I hold my breath and await his answer.

"If Noelle is to be found, your father has called the right source," he says in a matter of fact voice.

His gaze does not waver. I can see and feel his confidence. I can finally breathe again.

"I need a list of people who may have it in for you, Noelle or any of your immediate family," Asher says and reach for a note pad. He slides it out from the front pocket of his shirt, with his pen poised.

"I have only one enemy, which I can think of. His name is Victor Wallace!" I feel my chest clench painfully, when I think of Victor putting his hands on my wife and baby.

"Can you think of anyone else? We must investigate anyone and I mean anyone you can think of to have a vendetta against you or your family," Asher looks around the room, awaiting us to answer.

I think back to the day that Noelle gave birth to Brandon. I think of the scuffle between Victor and I, which led into an all-out fight. I think of the words he threatened. I can hear them as loudly as the day he said them in my head. I hear them over and over again, as I go back to that day…to the day, I now wish I had killed Victor with my bare hands. The thoughts from my mind floods upon me and carries me back to that awful day in the hospital…

"Wallace, didn't I tell you to stay the fuck away from my wife! How the hell did you get through security anyway," I ask him between gritted teeth.

"That's my baby in there and the woman that I love. Victor yells out angrily.

Blood rushes through my head and I begin to lose all reason. He dares to lay claim to my woman and baby. I don't think so.

"Beau!" I can hear Shelby call my name but I can think about is beating Victor's face to a pulp.

"Stop it! The both of you," the doctor shouts in a loud demanding tone. This is neither the time nor the place for this type of behavior," he continues.

My back is to him and my anger is too far gone.

"You better listen to him," Victor says with an evil glare in his taunting eyes. "That baby is mine, you have absolutely no business laying claim to my son. Noelle and I made our baby together and if I have anything to do with it, we will raise him together."

"The hell you say!" I charge straight at Victor, like a bull seeing red.

Victor throws up his arms like a defensive lineman blocking a defensive back, but I dip to the side, push Victor's elbow down and away. I grip his head in a headlock. I pay no heed to the excitement and loud voices around us. I roll Victor to the floor, which is no easy feat, since we are both muscle bound men.

Once full body contact is made, I begin to pound Victor's face with my fist. I take out all of my bitter anger on the man that impregnated my beautiful angel, then threw her away to fend for herself. I beat him for not being the man he should have for Noelle and I beat him for ruining what should've been the most wonderful moment between husband and wife but he ruins it.

"Stop it Beau! Noelle needs you," cries Shelby with a teary voice.

"Damn you to hell Victor," I ignore Shelby's pleading voice. I now have a death grip around Victor's fucking throat. Victor quick jabs me in my face, as he tries to deflect my grip from his corded throat. I feel no pain.

My hands are like an iron vise around his neck and I won't be satisfied until Victor expels his last breath. I can hear running feet in the hallway, before I feel a hand at my shirt collar, trying to force Victor and me apart.

"Let him go!" A man's voice orders.

"Let go of me!" I force out between gritted teeth as I struggle to hold on to Victor's neck.

"What the hell is going on here?" A voice booms from behind me. "Get your hands off of my son or I swear by God, I will have your job," states Billy Barringer, my father.

"Oh, my God!" I hear mother's voice cry out. "Beau, stop it, we didn't raise you to carry on like this. Noelle needs you."

"Beau," Noelle's voice is the only voice that penetrates through my mad haze. My hands loosen their grip. I fall back away from Victor. I breathe in and out heavily, trying to catch my breath. My father reaches out his hand in an offer to help me to my feet. I allow him to assist me, before turning towards Victor.

I watch Victor tries to get up on his own, but he fails miserably. Two security guards lifts him to his feet. He stands there and glares at me with hatred. I glare at him with equal hatred, for there is no love lost between the two of us.

Victor stance still holds defiance as struggles to catch his breath. "You will pay for this, Beau Barringer. Mark my words, the day will come that you rue the day that you put your hands on me. I can promise you that!"

"Get him the fuck out of here!" I order the two security guards.

"I'm sorry sir... We didn't realize it was you, Mr. Barringer! I don't know how he even made it to this floor. He didn't come pass us on the elevator; I can promise you that," says one officer, giving me a star struck look.

"How the hell you going to take his side?" Shouts a disgruntled Victor. You are going to pay for this Beau Barringer. I promise you will pay! Everything you think you've stolen from me will one day be mine again. I swear this on my life!" He yells with a crazy look of a lunatic in his eyes.

"Just get him the hell out of here!" I order. I'm so angry that fury radiates through my voice.

"Beau, Beau!" I finally come back to the presence. Hunter is calling my name. He is standing over me, with a look of concern on his face.

"Victor Wallace has my wife and son. I know this to be true for a fact. He threatened to get back what he thought belongs to him. I don't know how he did it or how he got into our home to do it, but he made good on his promise. I know where he lives. I'm going to kill him," I jump from my seat with deadly intent on my mind.

"Beau, I must caution you, if this Victor Wallace does have you family. I must warn you, by you going in without careful planning can and will work against you. You can make things worse off. We don't know the frame of mind, her alleged captor is in..."

I cut Asher off. "Alleged! Why do you say alleged?" I ground out between clenched teeth. We are wasting precious time. I need to get to my wife.

"Sit down Beau! Do you want to get Noelle and my grandson killed?"

I look at my father with shock in my eyes. How dare he suggests such a thing? I feel like no one understands my need to save my family. No one understand that I am slowly dying inside the longer that I am away from them. No one...not a one, I tell myself.

"Come on big brother," Hunter urges me back to my seat. "Listen to Asher. He knows what he's doing. We all want Noelle and Brandon home safe where they belong. We love them too," he states in a serious tone of voice.

Hot tears gather in my eyes. I do nothing to quench them. I allow them to run renegade down my cheeks. My shoulders tremble and the pain that overtakes me is unbearable. I know I need to be strong but in this moment, all strength has abandoned me.

My wounds are open for the world to see. My heart won't soften until the love of my life returns to me. I can't even think how alone and frightened she must be. Because, I feel just as afraid and alone. In this moment, I wish the earth to open up and swallow me whole.

I slowly come out of my pitiful musings to overhear the end of what Asher is saying. "I'm going back to your house. My credentials will get me in. But first, I want to talk with the security guard that was on duty, the evening that Noelle and the baby disappeared. I will keep you abreast of my findings. In the meantime, let me and the police do our work. Between the NYC police department and me, I assure you, your family will be home with you soon," he says before walking out of the room. His words left me with a mustard seed size of hope...A hope that will grow full bloom, when my family is found safe and sound.

CHAPTER 23
Noelle

I wake to the caress of Victor's hand on my thigh. I am sicken by his touch but am too afraid to scream. I don't know what he will do to me or my baby if he finds out what his touch really does to me.

I try not to stiffen up and breathe as normally as possible. Maybe he will go away soon, if he thinks I am asleep. Brandon, takes this inopportune moment to cry from his baby bed. My eyes pops open and stares into a strangers eyes.

For Victor is like a stranger to me. He is so far separated from the man, I thought I once knew. He is evil...I can feel this to the very morrow of my bones.

"Good morning beautiful," he says, with his hand inching up my thigh.

My jean clad legs closes automatically, to keep his hand from reaching the juncture of my thighs. "My baby is crying Victor. I need to go to him," I say before attempting to rise.

"You do mean our baby, don't you? When are you going to get it through that thick scull of yours, that this is our baby?" He suddenly screams.

Hot spittle from his foaming mouth lands hotly against my cheek. "I'm sorry, Victor. I don't know what I'm thinking. You are right. Brandon is our baby." My survival skill has kicked in. My brain warns me to comply with Victor as much as possible, so I can keep my little innocent baby safe.

I know by now Beau is looking for us. He has to be. If he can't get a hold of me by phone, I know he has contacted Shelby and his family, to question them of my whereabouts. I have to hold on to this fact, that Brandon and I will soon be rescued, if I am to keep my sanity. I have to remain strong for my baby. It doesn't matter how much, I want to break apart at the seams, I try to convince myself.

"Go, shut him up!" Victor screams down at me, before he roughly grasps my arm and lift me from the bed. "Now be a good mother and take care of our son!" He pushes me over towards the baby's crib. I almost stumble but rights my footing in time.

Tears dims my eyes when I look down at Brandon. He stops crying instantly when his eyes takes in my face. I reach down and lift him from the crib and hug his close to my chest.

"Mommy is here," I croon to him, against his soft wavy head of hair. I breathe in my baby's sweet powdery scent.

"I'm going to tend to breakfast," Victor finally says, before leaving out of the room.

I can finally breathe a sigh of relief, since he's no longer in the room. I freshen up Brandon from the small sink in the room and change him into a fresh diaper. I place him back in his crib for a moment to get his bottle ready for feeding.

By the time my baby is done with his feeding and burping, Victor comes into the room, laden down with a breakfast tray. He places it on a small table in the corner. There are two matching wooden chairs arranged at each end of the table.

"Breakfast is ready for my Queen," Victor gives me a big smile. There are no signs of the anger left in him which he blatantly displayed earlier.

I don't understand how his temperament goes from one extreme to the next in an instant. There is something terribly wrong with him and he needs to seek the help of professionals. But I dare not tell him this. Crazy people are always the ones who think they are the sanest, I muse to myself.

By the time place a satisfied Brandon back in his crib and reluctantly walk over to the table, Victor is holding my chair out for me to be sit down. "Thank you," I say and pretend this situation is normal, when it's as far from normal as it gets.

"You're welcome, darling," he reply and place a kiss on top of my head. I cringe inwardly on the inside.

Victor picks up his fork and attack his breakfast with relish. I look down at my food and pray, it doesn't contain poison. Victor looks at me staring at my food. It's as if he is reading my mind.

"I haven't poisoned your food, Noelle. I can't do that to the mother of my child, who I love to death," he reads my unspoken thoughts and say them aloud.

"I don't," I start to say. But he cuts me off.

"Don't lie to me," he points his fork at me as he holds it up in mid-air. "You must learn to be truthful about such things. You see what that white man has turned you into? You used to not be such a liar Noelle." He says, before he begin to eat his food again. "Not eat!" He orders, with a sinister look onto his once handsome face. Now all I see when I look at him is a psychotic demented individual.

"I'm not lying Victor. I'm just not too hungry this morning. My stomach is troubling me," I say, trying to calm the trembling of my body.

Victor's hands comes down hard on the table. I jump in my seat from his sudden explosive behavior. He hits the table so hard that the dishes rattle. "I slave over the stove this morning to prepare you a wonderful breakfast and you're not going to eat it! You are one ungrateful bitch," he adds getting up from the table.

"You're going to eat, if I have to force feed you myself," he glares at me. I notice how his hands clench and unclench into fists, in his rage. I pray that he doesn't hit me.

I hurriedly pick up my fork and choke down the food on my plate. I swallow the bits of food, along with the acidic bile that is attempting to rise in my throat.

"Now, that's more like it," Victor settles down in his chair once again. He lets out a deep breath, before he speaks again. "You do know how much I love you right?" He asks.

I nod my head yes, because I am too choked up to speak or force the words from my lips.

"I want you to say you love me too," Victor says.

I know that I must force myself to say the words, Victor wants to hear. The life of my baby and mine may depend on it. "I love you Victor. I always have loved you," I add for extra effect.

"I knew it!" He replies. "I have always felt you still love me and not him," he says speaking of Beau. "He can never satisfy in the way that I can," he continues as a look of lust enters his eyes.

My heart thumps so hard against my chest. Oh, God, please don't let Victor rape me," I say over and over again in my head. Because there is no way that I can freely give myself to him or any other man again.

Victor licks his lips and continue to rake his eyes over my body. His look alone makes me feel sordid and violated, even without him physically touching me once.

"I can't wait to make love to you again and make you mine. I'm going to make you forget Beau Barringer has ever been inside of you. I'm going to stamp him the feel of him from your body and replace it with mine." He states in a matter of fact voice.

I look down at the table. Hot salty tears leaks onto my plate. "Beau save me, before it's too late. Save us! My heart cries aloud…hoping against hope that somehow Beau hears my heart crying out to him.

CHAPTER 24

Beau

I toss and turn through the night, as I attempted to sleep in my old bedroom, at my parents' home. I wake up in a cold sweat with the sound of Noelle's voice calling my name. I doubt I've had two hours of sleep during the course, since being home.

There is a tentative knock on my door. "Come in," I say.

Bethany enters the room and roll in a breakfast tray. The aromatic smell of strong black coffee permeates my nostrils at once. I am going to need plenty of black coffee to get me through the hours of this day, I think to myself.

"Good morning Beau," Bethany says in greeting.

"I don't know how good of a morning it is but morning," I reply.

Bethany looks at me with pity in her eyes. She doesn't speak on the situation of Noelle, but I know it weighs heavily on her mind like the rest of us.

"Your mother and father wants you to get dressed and come down stairs, after you've eaten. They told me to inform you that there will be a news broadcasting at ten, this morning and all of you are expected to attend. Oh! And Noelle parents arrived earlier this morning. Your mother insisted they stay here instead of a hotel. She sent her driver to the airport to bring them here on arrival," she states me in great detail.

"Thank you Bethany. I will be down as soon as I get dressed. Will you tell them that for me?"

"Of course. If there will be nothing else, I will be on my way," she reply and take her leave.

I arise from the bed and pour me a cup of the strong black coffee. I don't have an appetite for food but I know I must attempt to each something if I don't want run the risk of getting sick. I also realize, I must keep up my strength.

I finish up with breakfast in no time at all and walk into the bathroom to take a shower. The duration of my shower, I keep hearing Noelle calling my name over and over again. My tuition is telling me that our love is keeping us connected and she's calling out to me to find her.

My heart shatters, because I feel at a lost right now. I feel like going against Asher's warning and confront Victor on my own. But if I bring more harm to my family by not acting rationally, I will never forgive myself.

The piercing pain from my tortuous thoughts strikes me with a heaviness that knocks me back against the slick shower walls. I slide down against the wall and let the hot water beat heedlessly against my pain wrecked body. Gut wrenching sobs proceeds to escape my body. The water continuously cascades and mixes with my salty tears.

I cry because a piece of my soul and heart is missing. It will never be whole again until my love and son is in my arms once again...

***

I walk into the drawing room and my parent's along with another couple are sitting talking in deep discussion.

"Beau," my mother spots me after I enter the room. "Come and meet Noelle's family, she says in a cordial tone of voice.

My eyes goes immediately to the couple who stands and greet me, with a look of apprehension in their eyes. I almost stop in my tracks when I look into the eyes of Noelle's mother. It is like looking at an older version of Noelle, herself. Now, I see what lovely vision of loveliness, Noelle will undoubtedly be in twenty five or so years.

"Beau, this is Mr. and Mrs. Nichole and Terrance Roberts, Noelle's parents," my mother makes the introductions.

"Hello Mr. and Mrs. Roberts, I extend my hand in greeting.

"There is no need to be so formal. You may call me Nichole," she says, before stepping forward to give me a hug.

"And you may call me Terrance, young man," says Noelle's stepfather, before giving me a solid handshake.

"I'm so sorry that we are meeting for the first time under these circumstances," Nichole says retaking her seat. "It's no secret I know that Noelle and I are estranged and has been for years. All of the blame lies at my feet," she admits.

'No, the blame lies at both of our feet," Terrance, speaks up.

"I always say, leave the past in the past," My father jumps into the conversation. What matters now is bringing Noelle home and reuniting her with all of her family."

Nichole Winters Roberts, begins to sniff. Her eyes water up with tears and begins to spill down her cheeks. It breaks my heart to even look at Noelle's mother in tears. It's amazing of how much she and Noelle looks alike.

"If only I can go back in time. I would do things so differently, she says. I just pray to God it's not too late to make it up to her for not being there as a mother for her during her years.

"You will get the chance to make it up to her. Noelle and your grandson, will be coming home to us very soon," I state adamantly.

Hunter, Madison, Shelby and Erick enters the room, after my claim.

"You're damn right she's coming home soon," Shelby says coming into the room. "I had a dream about Noelle last night. She was holding two little babies in my dream. Beau, you were standing over her and smiling. I know this dream speaks of the future and I'm holding on to that fact," she continues with a voice of hope.

"That is truly a beautiful dream, Shelby," my mother speaks up. She then makes the introductions of the others that enters the room.

Shelby looks at Noelle's mother with a look of disdain and contempt. "Yes, Noelle has told me all about you. It's amazing how much your daughter looks like you and she has a heart of gold instead of a heart made of stones," she says in an insulting voice.

"Shelby! My mother gasps aloud. "I'm sorry Nichole…Shelby happens to be your daughter's best friend."

"I'm more than Noelle's best friend," Shelby cuts my mother off. "Noelle is the sister that I've always wished for but never had. My parent's loves her like their own daughter. They are going through hell right now with worry that she and her son are missing. They are offering a five hundred thousand dollar reward for her safe return. What are you offering?" She asks, looking directly into Noelle's mother's eyes.

"That's enough Shelby, Erick says with a stern tone. "Mr. and Mrs. Roberts, on behalf of Shelby and myself, I offer you both of our sincere apologies."

"I understand," replies Nichole. "Shelby has every right to speak her mind. The truth hurts and I have to live with my wrongness. From here onward, all I can ask for is my daughter's forgiveness, when I see her again. And I will have the chance to see her again, right Beau?" She asks with a tearful voice.

"Right," I answer. I'm hoping that what I say is the truth.

"The cars are waiting to take us to the press conference, my brother Hunter states.

"Well, we better be off then," my father stands and urges us to get ready to leave.

My cell phone goes off on the way out of the door. I hang back, but motion them to go on out the door. I will catch up with them momentarily.

"Hello," I speak into the receiver of my cell phone.

"Beau Barringer?" The voice inquire on the other end.

"Yes, this is him," I reply.

"This is Asher Vallencourt. I need you to meet me right now," he says getting straight to the point.

"Where are you?" I ask, feeling a chill run down my spine.

"I'm in the park across from Victor Wallace's, house. I've been having someone watch his apartment building ever since you told me of your suspicion. A couple of people has also been questioned. No one saw anything. But this little old lady says, she saw Victor carry in a bundle wrapped in a sheet into his apartment on the night of the storm. She says, he went into the apartment and stayed for about two minutes before going out again. She says, he had a large wicker basket in his hands and went back into his apartment again and she hasn't saw him since."

"We need to call the police ASAP!" I snap out and walk out the door.

Hunter, walks up to me on the way out the door. "I'm on my way, Asher," I say before ending the call.

"What does Asher want?" Hunter asks me.

"Get the family to go on to the press conference, but I need you to come with me. I will explain along the way, I tell him. "Wait for me by the truck. I will be right back," I say not waiting for Hunter's response, I double back into the house to my father's study, for some much needed back up in case I need it.

CHAPTER 25

Noelle

"You have got to see this," Victor says strolling into the room with a happy smile on his face.

How can he be so happy, when it seems I'm experiencing a living hell? Each moment apart from the man I love, breaks me a little more...hour by hour and day by day. I muse to myself.

Victor goes over to a wall across from me and slides back a compartment to reveal a hidden television screen. I'm surprised to see the television behind the hidden compartment. I had no idea it was even there.

He clicks it on with the wireless remote. The same remote, he uses to open the prison room doors, which he holds me and my baby captive. An ongoing press conference floods the television screen.

"Hello everyone, my name is Troy Bryant and I'm the lead investigator working on the mysterious disappearance of Noelle Winters Barringer and her son. Brandon Barringer. If anyone has seen this woman and her infant son, please get in immediate contact with the telephone numbers on the screen."

The investigator holds up a ten by ten glossy photo for the world to see. That is the last picture I took with Brandon, a few weeks ago, I think to myself. I look over at Victor and he is savoring every word that comes out of Troy Bryant's mouth. He is one sadistic bastard, I think to myself. I turn back my attention to the television screen…I'm in hopes that I will get at least a glimpse of my husband's loving face.

"The FBI has been called in on the case, since the victims have been missing over forty eight hours. I want to assure you the NYC police department or the FBI are taking this case lightly. The perpetrator or the perpetrators will be brought to justice and held in accountability to the fullest extent of the law," Troy Bryant, continues to talk into the microphone on the platform provided.

"Ha! They can look for you all they want. They will never find you. The police have already been here and looked around. They found nothing!" Victor says and throws his head back in laughter.

I feel red hot anger boiling through my blood. I am close to losing it, even though my safety and the safety of my baby may be at risk. But I am slowly coming t realize that death will be better than to spend the rest of my life with this crazed man.

"Why do you torture me so, Victor? I find my voice to say.

"Pfft! He makes an absurd sound with his mouth. This is nothing, compared to the torture you've given me by marrying that man," he says with anger in his voice.

"Victor, you had moved on with Samantha and your son. I thought," I didn't get to finish my sentence. Victor is up like a flash and standing in my face.

"Don't you ever bring up that bitch's name again! Before I know what happening. Victor backhands me against my mouth, with the force of all the rage that's within him.

I cry out in pain as he catches me by surprise. He bends at the waist and peers evilly into my eyes. Before I know it, he twists my long curly hair around his hand and grips it painfully.

I can feel blood trickle from the corner of my mouth, where his hand made contact. "You will learn to obey me. Is that understood?" This demon of a man glares down at me.

I am more frightened than I've ever been in my life. I didn't think that is possible until this very moment. He forces my head to shake up and down, to agree with him.

"That's a good girl," He says before sticking out his tongue to lick the blood from the corner of my mouth.

I fight the bile that rises in my throat, as he pushes me away suddenly. My back lands against the cot. I sit up and scuttle my back against the wall. I thank God that Brandon is sleeping. I had fed and changed him thirty minutes earlier and he will be down for a couple of hours, before he wakes again.

Victor, walks off and sits in a chair and gives the television screen his undivided attention. It's as if he forgets his anger and is once again his old self.

"I'm leaving the floor open for a few questions. Go ahead and ask your question, Troy Bryant points toward a reporter.

"Was there a break in and if so did there appear to be a sign of any struggle?" Asks the reporter.

"Yes, we can say, there was a break in and there appears to be no sign of a struggle," he answers the reporter.

Camera flashes everywhere as more reporters tries to get their questions answered.

"You there in the back, the green striped shirt. You may go ahead with your question sir," directs Troy.

"Is it possible that a lunatic fan of rock star Beau Barringer has something to do with his wife's and son's kidnapping or maybe a disgruntled ex-boyfriend," the reporter continues.

"We've talked to everyone that ever had any connection with Mrs. Barringer. No one seems to know of anyone who can have a possible grudge against her or her family, at this point," Troy Bryant goes on to say.

"But isn't it correct that if you do have a suspect in your sights, you can't give out that kind of information on the air, in case the suspect or suspects will take off?" asks a very astute reporter.

"That is correct mam. We have time for only one more question before we bring her family forward to speak. You, in the blue dress, ask your question," the investigator says.

"Did anyone see anything in the neighborhood on the evening in question? And how the hell is anyone of us can feel safe if someone was taken from a gated community? The news reporter asks.

"I did say one question but I will answer both questions," replies Troy. "First off I will say, no one in the neighborhood saw anything suspicious. But in light of the hurricane sweeping through our area that day, I'm sure everyone was indoors, trying to stay safe. The city had a statewide emergency warning in place and I'm sure anyone with common sense, was taking heed to that warning."

"All but the suspect," someone from the crowd shouts out.

I notice investigator Troy, ignores the wise crack spoken aloud and continue to speak. "It appears that the lines of the security system and the monitors were cut, which leaves no evidence of who did this monstrosity. Now, I want to bring her family forward to say a few words," he beckons my family up to the podium.

I gasp aloud, when I see my mother Nichole Roberts and my stepfather Terrance with the Barringer's. I see everyone that I have come to love and think of as my extended family. My best friend Shelby and Erick are also there. I also notice Madison is there but not Hunter. I see everyone else but who I crave to see the most. I don't see my husband...my soulmate Beau. In that instant my heart breaks like precious glass and shatters into a million pieces.

"Ha, ha, ha," Victor laughs aloud. Where is your precious Beau Barringer? I told you he doesn't love you the way I do. He don't think you're worth it to fly back to the States. He's probably holed up in some expensive hotel fucking the shit out of Courtney Nicks," he reveals his thoughts to me, with satisfaction written across his face.

I hold my lips together in a tight line and bite back my reply. I don't dare want to feel the wrath of Victor's anger again, anytime soon.

"Beau Barringer is pathetic! He makes me sick. And give me that ring," he snatches my finger up and twists off my wedding ring set. You don't need these anymore," he spits out.

My hand feels naked without my beautiful wedding set Beau gave to me. The same wedding set, I promised him, I will never take off. Victor holds my diamond encrusted wedding set in his hand tightly. The sharp diamonds cut through the palm of his hand. Blood drips onto the floor from his hand but he seems oblivious to it, as he directs his attention back to the television screen. I direct my attention as well, for the sight of his blood, turns my stomach.

"Please, I appeal to the human decency of whomever have my daughter and grandson…please release them," My mother Nichole pleads.

I have never saw her look as broken as she looks right now. Her words seems to be sincere as she stands there with tears gracing her cheeks. She continuously pleads for my safe return.

By the time Shelby walks up to the microphone and stares directly into the television screen, fat tears are squeezing from the corner of my eyes. "Noelle, if you are watching this…know that each of us loves you and are praying for your safe return. I miss you and my god baby. We will leave no stone unturned, until you and your baby are safely home." Shelby remains strong until her last words are spoken. Her voice cracks and Erick gathers her in his strong arms. I can visibly see her small shoulders wracking with tears.

"That bitch needs to sit her ass down somewhere. She doesn't give a damn about you. I don't know why she pretends to. And your mother with her fake crocodile tears, gets on my last nerves," he says with his back to me. He never takes his eyes off of the television screen.

I glance at his back pocket. The little black remote is sticking out his back jean pocket a bit. I look around the room to see if I can find something...anything steady enough to knock Victor in the head to knock him out. I think will I have enough time to get Brandon and make a dash for freedom.

"What are you thinking about?" I am so deep in thought; I didn't realize that Victor switched of the television. I didn't realize he is now staring at me with an intense look on his face.

"I...I am just thinking about how right you are," I lie. I think you're right, when you say no one loves me but you. Beau, didn't even love me enough to plead for my safe return during the press conference," I reply with tears leaking from my eyes like a running spring. In truth, my heart is broken for Beau's absence at the press conference.

"If what you say is true, stand up and take your clothes off," he orders.

My heart plummets at Victor's demand. I lose my voice momentarily as I try to think...to think of anything that will hold him off me. "The baby, is in the room. I can't do it with the baby in the same room," I tell him.

Victor walks over to the baby bed and looks down at Brandon. He stands over him for a minute, before he turns back towards me. "The baby is asleep and we will keep the noise level to a minimum."

I chew nervously at my bottom lip, while I'm trying to think of some plausible excuse which Victor will listen to. Out of a sudden, he snaps his fingers, as if he's having a revelation.

"I know what you need. I have a bottle of wine in the pantry. It will help loosen you up. I will be right back...get comfortable for me," he says with a wink and stroll out of the room. He makes sure he shuts the door behind him.

I immediately get up and walk over to the seamless door. I feel up and down the wall, trying to find an opening. I find none...I hate to do it, but I am desperate. I walk over to the baby bed and lift Brandon in my arms. I pepper sweet kisses on his face to rouse him from his deep sleep. He slowly wakes up and his tiny body begin to squirm in my arms.

"That's a good baby," I whisper. "Wake up for mommy," I continue to whisper against his soft neck. Brandon sounds off an alarming wail, by the time Victor enters the room with a bottle of wine in an ice bucket. He also has two wine glasses in his hands.

He leaves the door open and my eyes zero in on the open door. "Damn!" He mutters out. Can't you shut him up? He's ruining my vibe," he says before sitting the ice bucket on the small table in the room.

"That's what I'm trying to do," I lie. "I think he has a temperature," I tell another lie. "He needs some infant Tylenol. That will knock him out like a light," I want Victor gone, so I can devise a plan of escape.

"It's a store around the corner. You're lucky I'm feeling in a generous mood," he mutters under his breath. "When I get back, I will have you or else," he threatens before leaving the room.

I kiss my baby and hold him close. I look at the unopened bottle of wine and wonder if it's heavy enough to bring a man Victor's size down. I've seen it done on the movies. I just hope it proves true for me.

The End

CHAPTER 26

Beau

"I've waited long enough to confront Victor. The evidence you've gathered leaves no doubt in my mind that Victor has my wife and daughter. I'm going to beat the shit out of him, until he reveals their whereabouts," I say to Asher and Hunter.

Hunter and I have joined Asher Vallencourt in his surveillance of Victor's apartment building.

"No, you can't move too soon. That's Victor's car parked right over there," Asher points out.

"Whatever you want to do," I got your back brother," says Hunter as he gives me a pat on my back.

"Hey guys! Victor Wallace is on the move. He's just exiting the building," Asher says, getting our full attention as we watch from across the street.

Sweat begins to slide down my temple. My hands clenches and unclench against my sides. I can feel my heartbeat thumping in my ears as my blood begins to boil. If Victor has everything that I hold dear to my heart in his possession, I shall kill him, I silently promise myself.

"Beau, I'm taking your truck to follow him. I will be discreet about it," promises Hunter.

"Great idea. Call us of his destination," Asher instructs Hunter, after I give him my keys.

"Will do," Hunter replies, before jumping into my truck and taking off, behind an unsuspecting Victor.

"Where are you going?" Asher calls after me as I take off across the street.

"Where the hell do you think I'm going?" I tell him with impatience in my voice.

"Wait up! I'm going with you. Give me a sec," he instructs, before climbing into his surveillance van to get something. I can see him sliding something black into the back of his jeans, before he catches up to me.

"Let's go," I tell him and take off at a sprint across the semi-busy street.

Hunter is right behind me. Luckily someone is coming out of the building and we slip inside of the open doorway. I stop just inside the doorway, when I realize, I don't know which apartment Victor occupies.

"Victor lives on the first floor. Fifth apartment on the right," Asher answers my unasked question.

"Good looking out," I tell him and takes off at a sprint once again. Stand back," I direct Asher, as I get ready to kick Victor's apartment in.

"Asher places a strong hand on my shoulder to stop me from kicking in the door. "I don't think we need to kick down the door. I have the tools to get us in," he reassures me.

I don't argue with him. I step aside and allow him to work with his tools. If he takes too long in getting us in, then we will get in by my method, I say to myself.

"In under a minute, I hear a loud click, before Asher is opening the door. He quickly punches in a code to the alarm system beside the door. The red lights on the alarm, ceases to blink.

"You look around in the bedrooms and I will look around up here," Asher, say.

I nod my head in compliance and walk down the hall towards Victor's bedrooms. There are only two bedrooms in the apartment. One is a master's bedroom. The other bedroom is much smaller. I walk into the smaller bedroom first. I look under the bed and in the closet. This closet is empty except of some bed linens. There is nothing of suspect in this room.

I cross the hall and enter the larger bedroom. I know this is where Victor sleeps. The bed is unmade and his clothes are strewn over chairs and some lie in a heap in the corner of his bedroom.

I look under the bed but there is nothing under there. I go to his closet and look. I only see his clothes and some shoes lines a shoe rack in his closet. My cell buzzes at my hip. I reach for it and note Hunter's phone number on display.

"Beau," he speaks low like into the receiver of the telephone.

"Yeah, what's going on?" I continue to sweep the area of Victor's bedroom with my alert gaze.

"Victor is in a pharmacy, about twenty minutes from his apartment. He's purchasing some infant Tylenol," he says into the receiver.

A chilling thrill runs down my spine. Victor knows where my baby and wife are. Possibly they can be right under my nose and I just don't know it. Or possibly, he can have them hidden anywhere.

I quickly walk back through to the front of the apartment. "Asher!" I call out. "Hunter, stay on Victor. He may lead you to Noelle. Let me know where he goes next," I urge him.

"Okay, Beau. We will find your wife," he states before hanging up the phone.

"I'm in the kitchen," Asher calls out.

I follow the sound of his voice. He is bent looking through Victors trash can. His glove clad hands picks through Victor trash, piece by piece. He pulls a piece of balled up newspaper from the trash. The newspaper has a smear of red on it, which looks like blood.

"Is that blood?" I ask Asher.

"It seems to be," he replies. "It seems to have something hard inside," he adds.

I look on with curiosity as he opens the newspaper carefully. Something hits the floor. We both look down as a set of rings settles on the linoleum flooring, side by side.

I gasp aloud as I look on in surprise and then a feeling of trepidation befalls me as my eyes settles on the bloody newspaper in Asher's glove clad hand. Can that possibly be Noelle's blood, I silently question myself. I know I won't be able to withstand the answer, if it proves to be her blood.

"Wait!" Asher calls out to me but it is too late.

I stoop down onto my haunches to scoop Noelle's wedding ring set into my hand. I stand and fight back tears as I hold our promise of an eternity together, close in my heart.

"These wedding rings, belongs to my wife!" I scream this out in torture. I'm going to stay here until Victor returns. I'm going to beat him into an inch of his life until he tells me where my family is," I say emphatically.

"It's time to bring in the police and let them in on our findings. We need to get out of here before Victor comes home." He says placing the blood smeared paper into a plastic bag. "I need those rings too, for evidence," he says while holding the bag open for me to drop them into.

I hesitate before I make the decision to comply. My cell phone once again buzz at my hip. Asher is on his cell putting in a call to the police and asking for back-up.

"Hunter, it's him." I say of Victor. Victor has Noelle and my baby. I'm one hundred percent positive," I speak into the phone before he can say anything.

"I'm not surprised," he admits. He's heading back towards his apartment as we speak. We are less than ten minutes away." He states.

I become puzzled. "If Victor has Noelle hidden out and if he's getting Tylenol for the baby...Why is he coming back here? Something isn't connecting," I say and turn towards Asher.

Asher has a frown on his face. He is looking up at ceiling above the refrigerator. "Hunter, I need to go. Thanks for the heads up brother," I said ending the call, even though Hunter is telling me to get out of the building before Victor arrives.

"What are you looking at?" I ask Asher. I look up at the ceiling and upper wall but don't see anything amiss.

Asher doesn't say anything but he picks up a wooden chair from the kitchen table and places it on the side of the refrigerator. He takes a knife from his pocket and cuts through a thin wall. There are a bunch of wires connected together. He presses a button and the refrigerator pushes forward from against the wall. Asher hops down from the chair and we look at each other in total surprise.

I step cautiously and quietly into the room; the first thing I see is a baby's crib. It sits directly in the white washed room in beige undertones directly across from me.

"Oh my God, Beau!" I hear the sound of Noelle's voice from the area on my left. I turn towards her panic filled voice, to see her with a wine bottle held high above her head.

Asher rushes into the room, behind me at the sound of Noelle's voice.

"Noelle, my love," I look into her pale wan but still beautiful face. She still holds the bottle of wine in her clutches as the idea of seeing me tries to settle in.

"Is it really you, Beau?" She cries out.

"It's me baby," I say looking at her with disbelief in my eyes. I slowly ease the wine bottle from her grasp and set it aside.

"Oh, Beau!" She cries out and throws herself into my open arms.

"That bastard hurt you!" I say looking down at her swollen split lip. I will kill him, I vow to this to myself as hatred for Victor fills my heart to the brim.

I gather Noelle to me and my once dark soul is beginning to light up again. My lips settles softly on hers and sweeps her lips into a reuniting kiss as I try to kiss away her pain.

"Did he hurt you anywhere else?" I ask her, because I have to know.

"No, but I don't know how long before he did," she admits.

I embrace her to my chest once again. I never want to let her go. I never want to let her from my sight again. I settle my lips on hers once again.

"The baby Beau," Noelle whispers against my lips.

I pull my lips away from hers. My phone buzzes once again at my hip. I pay it no mind, as I walk with Noelle over to the baby's crib. Brandon eyes are open. He's the most beautiful baby in the world, I think to myself.

"Times is of the essence. Grab the baby and let's get out of here. We will let the police handle Victor Wallace," Asher voice urges us into action.

The first sounds of the police sirens can be heard in the distance, as we step into the kitchen from the prison of a room.

Noelle is at my side with the baby in her arms. Asher brings up the rear.

Victor Wallace charges in as if the hounds of hell are after him. He freezes in the doorway. The three of us freezes in our steps as well.

My first instinct is to push Noelle, behind me to keep her and the baby safe. My eyes keep Victor in my sight. Venom, begins to rise deep within me, when I see the man that took everything I hold dear from me. Until he feel the pain, which I feel from his misdeeds, I won't be satisfied to let him live.

"Get away from my woman and baby, motherfucker!" Victor barks out with a crazed look in his eyes.

I narrow my eyes at this lunatic. He didn't scare me one bit. Evidently crazy hasn't seen anything, from a man who will protect his family to the ends of this earth. Hell has no fury over a man like me, who will kill anyone for fucking with what belongs to me.

"Beau, the police will be here soon. Don't try anything foolish," Asher grates out in a low voice behind me. "You can get all of us killed, if you aren't careful. This man is unsettled, don't antagonize him further."

"He's right Beau. I've seen firsthand. Victor is truly off of his rocker," Noelle whispers behind me.

"I'm standing right here! I can hear you," Victor says and drops the plastic bag from his hand.

He reaches behind him and pulls out a gun. He points it toward us with a maniacal expression in his eyes.

"You don't want to do anything foolish," Mr. Wallace," Asher appeal to Victor in a calm voice. "You haven't hurt anyone as of yet. Just put the gun away, so that I can help you."

"I don't have beef with you, mister whoever you are. My beef is with this son-of-a-bitch right here!" He says pointing the gun right towards my heart. "If I get rid of him, Noelle and Brandon, will be all mine!"

I can feel Noelle's frighten presence trembling behind me. She lets out a loud whimper, which alerts me she is crying. Brandon must feel how upset his mother is because he begins to fret as well.

"I can get you the professional help you need, Mr., Wallace," Asher stills tries to reason with Victor.

Me personally, I have no time to reason with this fool. He has gone too far and caused too much damage. No one fucks with my family and live. My hand eases around my waistband. I make no sudden moves, but I slowly lift up the hem of my polo shirt and ease the forty five magnum from its hiding spot. I release the safety and point it directly at Victor's head. My shot will be clean and deadly. I'm dead on when it comes to hitting my target. I have been ever since my dad taught Hunter and me to shoot as kids.

"Drop your gun Victor," I gave him a warning

"Victor Wallace, come outside with your hands up!" Says a loud voice through a police bullhorn.

"You must die first, Beau Barringer," Victor screams before a loud pop from his gun goes off.

My right shoulder jerks back. I steady myself to regain my balance, because I know our lives hangs in the balance. Noelle screams and screams behind me. I can feel a scuffle behind me as Hunter yells for Noelle to hit the floor. I have no doubt, he will cover her and my baby, while I take care of Victor, even though I'm in pain.

I can feel an excruciating burning sensation ripping through my right shoulder. I look down to see and feel hot blood gushing through a hole in my shirt where the bullet tears through my flesh.

"All of you must die!" Victor's last vestige with sanity has totally deserted him. My shoulder is throbbing but I will it to lift at the right angle. I align my target in perfect sight. I don't dare let Victor get off another shot before I squeeze my own trigger.

Victor eyes widens in surprise as the bullet enters dead center between his eyes. The bullet penetrates cleanly…Victor body goes limp and drops to the floor. He is dead on impact.

The police rushes in. They order me to drop my gun. I obey. Asher, assists Noelle from the floor. "That's the suspect, right there, Asher comes forward.

"Make no sudden moves," the police urges as Asher reaches for his badge.

"I'm Asher Vallencourt; I'm the one who called in for back-up. If you will allow me to show you my I.D., I can shed light on this situation," he explains.

"Beau, you're hurt, cries Noelle. She falls into my arms. She doesn't care if my blood get on her own clothes it seems.

"I'm going to live baby. Don't worry," I try to embrace her and our baby in my good arm. I love you so much baby, I would die if anything ever happened to you."

"Sir, you need to see a doctor?" A young officer asks Beau.

"Yes he does," Noelle answers for me.

"An ambulance is on its way," he replies.

"Is he dead?" Noelle asks attempting to look over at Victor.

"Yes," I reply. "I had no choice."

"I know," she whispers as we embrace one another in the midst of all of the commotion that is going on around us.

"You saved us…I doubted your love for us more than once…I will never doubt your love for me or Brandon again…Her voice trails off, just before I place a gentle kiss on her lips.

I know from this moment on, even in the midst of such tragedy…Our lives will look up from this moment own. For Noelle Winters Barringer is my winter angel for all seasons to come. And I am her rock…her protector…the one that will love her and our family, even beyond the end of time.

EPILOGUE

The Future

(Christmas Day December 25, 2055)

Beau

"Noelle Barringer, I love you more than the first day I met you. You get more beautiful with each passing year."

"Hush old man," Noelle replies in a trembling voice but her eyes still twinkle with her youth of yesterday. "Look at this gray hair," she says patting the bun she has on top of her head.

"I'm looking woman and I know what I see when I look at you. I still see the bride that I carried over the threshold of our first home we built together forty years ago to this day," I place a kiss against her soft weathered cheek.

My blue eyes has paled over the years and my eyesight has dimmed but Noelle's beauty still shines as bright for me as the day I first met her all those years ago. I now walk with a cane because of my hip placement surgery but my heart feels as young and sprite because of this true beauty and the family she has given me through the years.

I reach over and dip my hand in the cake batter, she is whipping up. She taps my hand but it's too late as the mixture coats my finger and I bring it to my mouth to get a taste.

"Stop that," she reprimands me. "This cake batter has raw eggs in it."

"This batter is just as sweet as you are," I say and place a quick kiss on the back of her neck.

A door slams shut and we both look back as it gets our attention.

"Mom, Dad!" The voice shouts.

"We're in the kitchen kitten," I call out.

Bethany our youngest at the age of twenty seven enters the kitchen. Bethany is the replica of her mother but she has my dazzling blue eyes. She is our baby girl and never lets her older twin brothers Ethan and Evan as well as our oldest son Brandon forget it. Bethany being the only girl, you know her daddy had to spoil her a bit. It doesn't matter how old she gets, she will always be daddy's little kitten.

Brandon is really Noelle's and Victor Wallace's son but he thinks of me as my real father, just as much as if I had fathered him myself. It wasn't until he turned eighteen years old that we told him about Victor and what happened after he kidnapped him and his mom. We didn't want him to go off to college and find out from anyone else. We had been able to shelter him in private schools, until his senior year in high school. We knew once he went off to college, he would undoubtedly find out the truth. We felt it necessary for the truth to come from our lips and not anyone else's. Stories become false and embellished through the years. We gave him facts because that what he deserved. He listened to our side of the story. He said he didn't look at me any differently. He said I was the only father he knew and loved and he was glad that I was there to save him and his mom, when I did. That boy is after my own heart, I tell you, I muse.

"It smells delicious in here," Bethany walks into the room. She instantly pulls me away from my musings to the present as she gives each of us a hug and kiss. "What can I do to help?" She asks walking over to the kitchen sink to wash her hands and tie an apron around her waist.

"You can check on the turkey in the oven for me," Noelle reply.

"You got it mommy," Bethany answers.

The front door opens and slams again and loud voices can be heard.

"There goes my loud mouth brothers," Bethany sighs and rolls her eyes. "You would think they would have grown up by now, since each of them have wives and kids of their own."

Bethany always gave her older brothers a hard time because she always knows she can. Each of her brothers has always been just as protective about their only sister just as I have.

"Mom...dad," before Brandon and the twins come in here with their families...I have a friend that I invited to dinner. I really like him a lot. Please tell my brothers to not bully him and run him away like they do everyone else I bring home. I am twenty seven years old and it's high time I have a steady relationship in my life," she says in exasperation.

"Kitten, when you find a man that is deserving of you, won't nobody, not even me will be able to run him off. But I will talk to the boys before your friend gets here," I promise her.

Noelle looks back at me and make a clucking noise with her tongue. She already knows that I want do much to dissuade our boys behavior if we don't like the young man that Bethany has invited for dinner.

"Don't worry sweetheart," I can hear my wife whisper to our daughters. "I promise you, I won't let them run your young man off this time…It is high time we women in the family put these big bad wolves in their place," she adds with a chuckle.

"I love you so much mommy," Bethany voice trails off as the door to the kitchen shuts behind me.

"Granddad!" My five grandchildren run to me to bestow hugs and kisses to me.

Noelle and I have five grandchildren between our three boys. Brandon has a boy and girl ages five and seven. Ethan has a son age three and Evan has two daughters, ages one and four years old. Our family has grown and multiplied over the years and life has been wonderful.

Noelle and I have had our ups and downs over the years but we have always worked through them…just like the promises we made each other on our wedding day. A day I would live over and over again if I could.

"Where is mom?" Brandon asks. "I know Bethany is around because I see her car out front."

"I'm here," says Noelle as her and Bethany walks out of the kitchen.

"Merry Christmas mom," Our sons say in unison as they make a bee-line for their mother.

"Grandma!" Our grandkids shout as they make a bee-line for her as well.

Noelle happily receive the onslaught of hugs and kisses from our children and grandchildren. Her eyes and mine meet and the love radiates between the two of us just as much if not more-so as it did in previous years.

"I love you," I mouth.

"I love you too," she mouths back.

My heart swells with so much love for my wife and family. I am truly a blessed man beyond measure and I take nothing for granted on this Christmas Day or any other day. I am blessed…truly blessed and I have my beautiful family to prove it. Best of all, I get to have all of this with my Noelle still by my side in our glorious golden years that we will treasure for the rest of our lives.

To get exclusive and advance looks at some of our top releases:

Click the link: (App Store) http://bit.ly/2iYOdnZ

Click the link: (Google Play) http://bit.ly/2h4Jw9X

Join our mailing list to get a notification when Leo Sullivan Presents has another release!

Text LEOSULLIVAN to 22828 to join!

To submit a manuscript for our review, email us at

submissions@leolsullivan.com

CPSIA information can be obtained
at www.ICGtesting.com
Printed in the USA
LVOW10s2028030517

533142LV00015B/289/P